SLOW FIRE BURNING

SLOW FIRE BURNING

EIGHT STORIES OF ADVERSITY

Will Wyckoff

ISBN-13: 9781539914662
ISBN-10: 1539914666
Library of Congress Control Number: 2016918599
CreateSpace Independent Publishing Platform
North Charleston, South Carolina

Also by Will Wyckoff:

Birds on a Wire
Rabbit Trails

To my family
and those of you who kindly asked,
"When are you writing another?"
You are good for my ego!

CONTENTS

Acknowledgements

For me, it is not easy leaving family behind so that I may escape to what we [affectionately?] call *The Recluse Room*. That being said, my thanks goes to Kay, our kids, and our grandchildren for your patience.

To those of you who were helpful guides and sources, folks who provided facts, history lessons, corrections, and constructive criticism (Danika Stone, Bob DiGiallonardo, Don Sprague, Deborah Corcoran, Leyna Shaffer, Phil Hunt, Beverly Beck, Florence Simmons, and my parents Dorothy & C.T. Wyckoff), thank you for your individual contributions.

Then there are the contest winners! When I needed help creating titles for some of my stories, the following people came through in the clutch: Mary Lou Frisbie, Donna Ludwig, Sheila Becker, and Gail Wallat. A big thank you goes out to all of you!

As always, in keeping with tradition: Hi, Rupe! Hi, Mac!

PROLOGUE

꧁꧂

*"I wanted you to see what real courage is, instead of
getting the idea that courage is a man with a gun in his
hand. It's when you know you're licked before you begin,
but you begin anyway and see it through no matter what."*

— ATTICUS FINCH
— <u>HARPER LEE</u>, <u>TO KILL A MOCKINGBIRD</u>

ABOVE IS MY FAVORITE QUOTE from my favorite book. All I wish
to add is that I have witnessed acts of courage throughout my
life; so many different kinds of courage, too.

Perhaps the bravest thing I ever witnessed was the night
I said, "Love you, Fritz" to my father-in-law as I exited his
room in the ICU, and he calmly replied, "Love you, Will" as
if tomorrow was just another day. The truth of the matter is
that he suspected he would be deceased before sunrise. Such
a brave, selfless act.

I saw students defy bullies. I observed young adults with so much on their respective plates that I was certain they would be crushed, but they survived. At my request, one of my shyest students danced upon a classroom table at school year's end in front of a classroom full of peers. That, too, was courageous.

Therein lies my point, and it's nothing new. I am simply reinforcing an old idea: Courage comes in many shapes, flavors, and sizes. Given a situation, it might manifest spontaneously. But most of the time? I think we all have to dig deep, for within us courage can be a slow fire burning.

I wish you all the best. I know you will feel better for summoning your nerve when you must.

~ Will ~

A FLICKER OF MEMORY

✥

I wasn't at all threatened by his appearance in our neighborhood. Curious? Yes. Threatened? No.

IT IS SNOWING. TO THE background music of Bing Crosby's *White Christmas*, the pristine flakes seem to drift across the air outside my octagon window near the bottom of our foyer steps.

I have always wanted a house with a view, but it never came to be. Therefore, this particular window is my favorite in our entire home, for it provides an unobstructed view of the entire two and a half blocks down our tree-lined street across Main Avenue all the way to the theater. Our town's corner street lights illuminate the crooked, gnarled branches of each and every tree lining our sidewalks, for tonight they are decorated with ten inches of heavy, new-fallen snow.

"This is the kind of snow," I whisper to myself, "that could raise havoc with our electricity again." Losing power during a snowstorm is not that common, but during our thirty-five years on Keystone Street it is nearly a once-a-winter occurrence. All alone now, sitting here by the window, watching the snowflakes float by only inches away, I am reminded of a similar nighttime storm many years ago.

⊷⊲⊳⊶

"Honey!" my bride called to me from the foyer. "Come here for a second please." I found her sitting upon the fourth step leading up to our sitting room at the front of our house. She was staring out our octagon window.

"What's up?" I asked as I peeked curiously over her shoulder. She jumped a bit, for she was startled. I was at her side more quickly than she anticipated. Gently placing my hand upon her shoulder I asked, "What are you looking at?"

The end of her finger tapped the pane of glass that separated us from the chilly nighttime temperatures and a kajillion snowflakes that spangled our line of sight. Watching flakes drift by our porch light, she seemed mystified, but that was understandable for many were the times that snowfall had similarly entertained me as well.

As it turned out, I had not understood at all what held her attention. On this night, it had been captured by something far different. She wasn't tapping upon the window pane, she was pointing.

"I think I saw someone," Kathy informed me at last. She covered her mouth when she coughed a few times. I could hear her wheezing. "By his step, it appeared as if he was struggling. It's possible that if he was walking normally I might not have noticed him."

"Not to mention the fact that someone's even out on a night such as this." Then I added, "Anyone we know?" Through our window, I began to search the neighborhood in more earnest.

She tapped the window again, this time more emphatically. "There he is! See him?"

I stared in what I thought was the correct direction. I saw no one and grunted the same. To make her feel better, I continued to scan the street.

"No! Not in that direction, Silly." Kathy nodded her head to the right and tapped the glass one more time. "Down by the theater."

"The theater!" I countered with a little surprise in my voice. "You can make out a man's stride through all of this snow all the way down to the Ritz?" I tried some humor. "Where's your cape?"

She let out a disappointed sigh. "I don't know. I thought I did." She coughed, stood up, and announced that she was about to watch the evening news "…while the power's still on."

I stayed behind assuming her place upon the fourth step. I became the night watchman. "You think we might lose power?"

I heard her land in the recliner as she replied dryly, "It's been known to happen before."

I was able to hear the news broadcast, and little of it actually interested me, so I was able to be attentive while on sentry duty at our newest addition, my favorite window. Minutes later I, too, saw a figure seeming to struggle across the wide-open Main Avenue intersection. The scene was illuminated under the pale-yellowish glow of a pair of corner street lamps. I said nothing to Kathy, for I wanted to be certain.

As he came to within a block, the figure I spied seemed to be appropriately dressed wearing a large overcoat, a hood or scull cap, and what appeared to be taller boots. I couldn't see his hands, but it seemed he could have been sufficiently warm.

As for struggling? From what I was able to discern, the illusion of struggle came in the form of leaning against the buildings as he slowly passed them by. As Tarzan once advanced from one jungle vine to the next, this soul leaned against each fence or house as he slowly advanced toward our block. Yet because he did not attempt to peer into windows or jiggle any doorknobs on a single door, I wasn't at all threatened by his appearance in our neighborhood. Curious? Yes. Threatened? No. I continued my shift not sharing with Kathy what I had been witnessing outside on our street.

"Is it possible he is just out for a walk?" I asked myself. "If he is, he's quite adventurous." As the figure slowly continued upon his way up the sidewalk across the street from our front porch, he moved in and out of the shadows cast by the tall, snow-laden maple trees that have lined our block for decades. Perhaps the shadows were the culprit, adding mystery to all I witnessed which really wasn't much.

Most structures in our neighborhood are 150 years old or older, and are located right along our flagstone sidewalks. Local historians tell us this was done intentionally in order to offer residents more space for gardening. A few chose to do the opposite. They placed their homes at the back of their lots and gardened right out front.

The Hettinger House was one such structure two doors down from us, on the opposite side of the street, and though its garden was abandoned years ago, a hedge did grow tall in its place. The snow-covered hedges provided my wanderer no support at all, and it appeared they were difficult to negotiate. Making things worse, he stumbled into the thick, scratchy barrier that now circumvented the yard and was covered by snowfall from head to foot as a result. As he shook himself off, I could only imagine the cold.

Down the hall, the TV went silent, and the news anchor's voice was replaced with traditional Christmas tunes that always made me sentimental. I heard Kathy's slippers flip-flopping in my direction. Again she was coughing.

"See anyone?" she inquired.

"Uh huh," I replied trying to sound aloof. "Yup."

As if surprised by my calm admission, she blurted, "You did?"

In an attempt at a more subtle humor, this time I tapped my finger firmly several times upon our special window overlooking Keystone.

"Look at Hettinger's."

"Near the hedges?" She pressed her nose against the glass. "I don't...wait...I see him!" In an excited tone she followed, "Do you recognize him?"

Time for more humor. "Well I have narrowed it down a skosh. He isn't Santa Claus, and I suspect he's too large to be an elf."

Somehow Kathy wiggled herself between the window and me. Not an Olympic athlete by any means, I found it to be a tight fit as we sat together upon Step Number Four.

The figure across our street commanded our attention, for he seemed to be battling the inclement weather with greater difficulty.

"Why do you suppose he's out there?" she asked. "He's making me feel cold just looking at him."

"I'm wondering why he's not moving on," I replied. My sense of humor abated and curiosity was running only slightly ahead of worry. "I'm going out there," I announced. I made it sound as if there was not room for debate.

"You're what?" Kathy's reaction was clearly indicative of her disapproval. "What do you mean you're going out?"

I pulled my favorite dark brown winter coat, my gloves, and my hat from out of our foyer closet under our steps where we kept all of our winter apparel. "I think he's either in need of assistance, or he might be up to no good."

"Danard, I don't know..."

"Kathy, it does us no good to be in limbo...to not know. It's better if I investigate." I was finally stepping into my boots, about to swing open our door, and step outside into the storm. "Besides, what if he is in serious need of help?" With that being said, I finally opened the door, leaving my wife and the entire 1st U.S. Marines Carolers Unit behind.

Through the door I heard Kathy call out, "Be careful!"

Earlier that day, I had made the choice to clean off our walks after the storm had passed. As a result, I was forced to march atop twelve inches of wet, heavy snow finding it quite a slippery journey to the middle of the street. It was there my courage and my courtesy were matched by my fears. Standing in the middle of the road among the uneven ruts provided earlier by snowmobile riders, I called to whomever was there.

"Hello? Sir!" I stepped a bit closer. "Do you need my help?"

After I repeated my inquiry a time or two, I began to wonder whether or not this traveler was deaf. Wind was blowing flakes all about, but it I didn't think it made me inaudible. In fact, in the distance I could hear the voices of some raucous drinkers as they exited the McTool's on Main. Then I questioned *their* judgment being out on such a night. "Liquid courage," I muttered to myself. "Making ugly men handsome since 1828."

As I continued briefly to observe the scene playing out under the street lights of our main thoroughfare a block and a half away, I was alarmed by a reply that came from but a few feet to my right.

"I'm grateful for your—"

"Whoa! What the--"

"My my! I've startled you," were the words I heard next. He spoke in a higher than usual pitch, not nasally but hoarse. "I just wanted to thank you for checking on me."

I still couldn't see his face, but at least I was now reasonably sure we had been watching a man hike up our street, not a woman.

"How did you come upon me so quickly?" He was correct. He had alarmed me, for my heartbeat was just beginning to slow. "One second you were near Mildred's bushes," I added as I pointed toward our elderly neighbor's porch next to the Hettinger Place, "and the next second you're practically on top of me here in the middle of the road."

"Street."

"What?"

"Middle of the street. The street sign says, 'Keystone Street'," he added with a chuckle.

I didn't know what to think. I had stepped out from the comfort of our cozy home with the intention of offering help, and I found myself being tutored in local geography.

"Right. Keystone Street," I conceded. "It's slippery under foot. How did you move so quickly?" I was finally able to see his face, and it was covered with thick, gray whiskers that were temporarily home to a few white snowflakes.

Again he chuckled just loudly enough to be heard. Mixing it in with his speech, I felt as if I was listening to a happier soul who was not at all in any state of worry or emergency.

"Well you stood here quite a while observing those folks down on Main--"

"Avenue...Main Avenue." I felt compelled to show him I knew at least *that* much.

"That's right," he continued as we both looked in that direction. "Main Avenue." Then as naturally as the snow fell from the dark sky above us, as if it was an everyday occurrence, he took my arm with his gloved left hand, and with his right hand he graciously motioned toward our front door. "Shall we go in?"

I was invited into my own home by a man I didn't even know. He seemed so congenial that it was impossible to resist *his* hospitality. "Is Kathy taking in all of this?" I thought to myself.

As we approached our stone porch steps, he held on to my arm for safe footing which I thought was odd considering moments ago he seemed to float from the sidewalk across Keystone to my side in the middle of the ...street. Something else odd popped into my mind, something he said moments ago, so I inquired as we stood at the bottom step.

"How did you know I was 'observing those folks down on Main' to use your own words?"

Grabbing a hold of our black, wrought-iron railing he quipped as he turned to me, "What else could it have been?" Not missing a beat, he turned and was met by Kathy at our door. It turned out she *was* watching, and I made a mental note to later ask her what she had witnessed taking place between the two of us outside in the...street.

Almost rudely I stepped past our new acquaintance, for it was then that I realized I had yet to learn his name. Introductions were certainly in order. When I realized I didn't know his name, I guess I became protective of my queen. He beat me to the punch.

"Good evening, Kathy," he said as he reached the third and final step to our door. "It is my pleasure to meet you. I'm Nick." The manner in which he spoke couldn't have been more natural or more good-natured. His voice was jovial and gentlemanly. His manner immediately put both of us at ease. Mental note number two: Try to recall later whether or not I ever mentioned Kathy's name as we stood there in the... street.

"Well, Nick," she replied with no hesitation, "let's get these wet clothes off of you and have a cup of tea." I could tell by her amiable tone that he had won her over already.

❈

Soon it was eight o'clock which magically became nine and then ten. Over hot tea and homemade Christmas cookies, our trio exchanged many stories and information that made us all smile, made us laugh, and made us grateful to be sheltered from such a storm.

As it turned out, old Nick was and wasn't new to our town. Born "up north" as he put it, in the province of Alberta, we learned of such places as Lethbridge, Red Deer, and Wood Buffalo National Park.

He told us, "It's the second largest national park in the world." I was quite surprised for I had never heard of it.

"What's the largest?" I asked.

"Northeast Greenland National Park. I've flown over both and they're beautiful."

By ten o'clock, we had learned that Nick once raised and herded reindeer, helped push through legislation to protect the wood bison, and even earned a university degree in orienteering. "That's a skill that has been very useful throughout my various careers."

A smile came to his face as he seemingly was traveling down Memory Lane. "Actually my work has taken me many places including this wonderful hometown of yours." As best he could, he spoke of flying and how it helped him become part of philanthropic endeavors worldwide. He spoke of the many cultures he had experienced, too. "In a nutshell, I was part of a delivery system similar in design to Canada's Canpar and Purolator organizations, not at all dissimilar to FedEx or UPS.

"Still to this day," he told us, "there are cultures that have yet to witness small town or city life." His eyes widened as he shared tales of people having no concept of plumbing or electricity. "Our goal was not to alter their cultures at all, just to help them maintain their way of life in any way we could."

"And here I sit," I added, "worried we might temporarily lose power due to all this wind and snow."

Kathy had begun cleaning the few mugs and cookie dishes we used for our snacks as we chatted. Looking out our back window above our kitchen sink she commented, "It certainly has not let up at all." She coughed hard a few times, took down a glass from the cupboard, and poured a cold drink to help her find some relief.

I looked in her direction. Perhaps a life together improves telepathy, for when our eyes met I knew she was asking, "What now?"

Some processes are slow, and my thought process that evening was their rival. All of a sudden, I had an epiphany, and my words escaped my mouth before I could retrieve them.

"Nick, you have never explained why you were outside tonight." Ordinarily I am uncomfortable when it comes to prying into the business of another person's life, but his involved us. From the corner of my eye, I saw Kathy turn and lean against the sink, arms folded. She, too, was curious.

The old gent we had begun to call "Nick" just smiled, and for a moment he leaned back in his chair. Its spindles squeaked that wooden squeak that's heard when one shifts his weight even the tiniest bit upon a well-worn chair. Finally, he leaned forward placing his folded hands upon our table.

"I was looking for the two of you," and there it was. Simple. He was looking for us.

"Looking for us?" Kathy sat down and we, too, slid closer to our drop-leaf table.

"I was. Most certainly." Then he added, "It took me a spell, but here I am!"

"Why? Why would you be looking for us?" Now I was in full *blurt-it-out mode.* I continued, no longer inhibited. "And why on such a night as this?"

For the first time since Nick set foot in our house, I sensed he was about to become serious or maybe less light-hearted. He seemed to be choosing his words carefully. For several seconds and maybe even a moment he was quiet. Finally, he shared his reasoning.

"Danard," he began gently, "as it turns out, the two of you are well-respected in this community of yours." He gently held up his hand to request that he not be interrupted for he knew I was still in full *blurt-it-out mode*. "During my visits here, more than once I have encountered you in the local market and the diner. Whenever you departed, folks were complimentary of you both." He paused. "Let's just say that in my travels I hear things and observe things." Then he added, "I've formed many long-lasting connections as well."

Again, he shifted in his seat, but the result this time was different. No folded hands. This time he placed his left hand on Kathy's forearm.

"Kathy, the two of you don't know it, but that cough of yours is symptomatic of something far more dangerous than the common cold." Things grew quiet. "You are quite close to becoming seriously ill."

Our faces surely revealed our surprise at what we had just been advised. My reaction alone, if it had weight, would have put a barge asunder.

"Now wait just a minute!" I countered indignantly. "Are you a doctor? How *dare* you come into our home--"

I was interrupted. "Danard, it's true," my bride informed me in a soft voice that was strong and at the same time apologetic in tone. "I was going to tell you after Christmas. I didn't want to spoil our holiday." Her brown eyes became rheumy with her admission.

My eyeballs were attending a tennis match! I looked at her and immediately looked back at Nick. Then I looked back at Kathy.

I pondered nervously, "How much does he know?" and "How much does Kathy know?" I wanted to interrogate *someone*, and I didn't know how to begin.

Making things doubly difficult, I didn't know whether I should sound cross or concerned. Part of me was angry that Kathy had not told me, and a total stranger knew about all of this before I did. My flip side told me I should be grateful that our bearded, new acquaintance had brought the situation to light, and that I needed to step up by helping my wife, not make her feel worse. I opted for compassion. Just how Nick found out was inconsequential.

Finally, I asked, "What are we to do now? We are in this together." For the longest time, we sat quietly. All three of us heard the wind pick up and our old house creaking. The combination made for an ominous setting.

⊰⊱

All of that took place years and years ago, but to this day the details of that night are some that my old brain cannot shake. Nor do I want to do so.

A total stranger with a full, white beard entered our lives on the snowiest of nights. His name was Nick. He was from up north in Alberta and places beyond, and by the grace of international delivery, he was able to create and maintain a philanthropic network like no other I have known since.

As it turns out, he was right. Nick was right. Kathy indeed had become victim to the dreaded disease bronchiectasis, in which there is permanent enlargement of the airways in the lungs. Breathing becomes difficult quickly. People die. How old Nick came to know this is another story for another time. What is important is the fact that this man from the North learned someone was in need and was compelled to take action.

As I sit by the very same octagon window tonight watching yet another winter storm race by its glass, I am reminded of the fight Kathy fought until it was over. Treatments involving the most-modern antibiotics, several surgeries, and even a lung transplant never dampened her spirits, and all the while Nick and I were present by her side.

Yes, it's snowing, and I sit here alone upon the fourth riser next to the window. But I won't be alone for too long. From the kitchen I can hear her preparing some hot chocolate that we will sip together as we look down the …street and celebrate another wonderful Christmas thanks to our jolly, old friend Nick. The man truly is a saint.

FOG HOLLOW

⟡

About this time, the woods grew ominously quiet. It was
strange. Not a breath of air was on the move. It was eerie.

EVERY EVENING SEBASTIAN SAT NEAR the fieldstone hearth by the
fire. Each night his younger sister Loretta would awaken and
find him there upon the stool, seated in such a manner as
to borrow the blaze's glow for reading light. The fire would
crackle and snap while flames would cast dancing shadows
upon the cabin walls. Yet neither dancing light nor crackling
embers distracted him.

Without fail, Sebastian would somehow sense just when
she was watching. Her handsome brother would look upon
her across the space between them, and she knew during
those special moments that were theirs alone that she mattered to him. It was just his look; her brother's special look.

Daytime created yet another world in Fog Hollow. After
the morning mist lifted each day, life was bright, noisy, and

full of necessary chores. Like most colonial adolescents, Loretta had desires above and beyond her daily chores. Deep within her diminutive self she felt a pang and believed she would nearly burst if she could not get to the orchard before the others.

No child in the settlement had longer, golden hair, so when she was ten years old Sebastian nicknamed his sister "Goldy". After tying it back as best she could with one of the few ribbons she possessed, each and every morning Goldy was required to stack the kindling wood Sebastian chopped using a wedge and a sledge hammer to do so.

Mumbling unhappily as she worked, Goldy sometimes listened to her friends' voices off in the distant woods. It was a thick, thick forest of evergreens, maples, and birch that surrounded her family's clearing which they had recently begun to call their farm. Distracted by her friends' laughter, Loretta's focus occasionally drifted to thoughts of their merriment without her. At such times, she became momentarily careless and in her eagerness to join those already at play, she would mishandle the ponderous shards of wood she had tediously collected. If Sebastian witnessed her lapses, he would tease her endlessly, but he would always help her. He was just so kind.

Her most difficult daily chore involved their dog. Grooming Ootah was not so bad, but exercising him was not always easy. He was an excitable hound, and he was exceedingly strong. Squirrels and chipmunks would trigger his throaty bark, a signal that Loretta was about to be pulled forcefully wherever Ootah wished to take her. At moments such as these, her brother would howl more loudly than the dog! Yet always ... always Sebastian would catch up to them and allay her fears. Many were the days when her wonderful, older brother made it possible for her to join her friends and their far-away voices.

"Your brother spoils you," her mother would say firmly. Mother was a burly, hard-working, no-nonsense tyrant sometimes, but she understood and appreciated the kindness with which her son showered his sister. Since the death of her husband, Sebastian was her poultice.

"Nobody ever helped *him* with his chores when he was fifteen," her mother would say while Sebastian was out of earshot.

Eyes set toward the ground, Goldy would listen respectfully until she was finally permitted to trot off and join her friends. Mother believed her daughter should be aware of just how fortunate she was to have such a brother, and Mother reminded her daily.

In the orchard were several large boulders decorated by decades of lichen. It was upon the boulders where the kids liked to gather most and rest from running about. Sons and daughters of colonists had met upon them for years. It was from this location whence the friendly voices of the woods emerged.

Most days the girls would eventually seek their own piece of the orchard at the risk of catcalls and teasing cast at them by their young, male counterparts. This clutch of colonial ladies deemed themselves young women, and during these more private sessions discussed young men among many other topics. Loretta's brother always fared well in these discussions; not only because there were few young men in the settlement, but because Sebastian was an amiable, strong, good-looking young man.

One bright day in late summer when a hint of autumn rode the breeze, the girls excitedly spoke of a new family in Gravity, and part of that family was a young boy. His name was Ed Buckmaster. He knew none of the females in the area, but stories about him had reached the young women already.

"We saw him by the church," giggled a few of the girls. "He has such long, curly hair!"

During this gathering in the orchard, Loretta patiently listened to the other girls speaking of young Master Buckmaster. He was a novelty and interesting fodder for discussion, but eventually Loretta found herself talking to the others about Sebastian. They listened intently as she shared her true feelings for her older brother, and she was speaking kindly.

"Have you ever told him how you feel?" inquired one of the older girls. At this, a few more began to giggle, yet there was an air of attentiveness nonetheless. They anticipated an awkward reply.

"That's foolishness," replied Loretta as she blushed more than a little while looking at her friends around her.

"Why?" a few of the group shot back simultaneously. "Why is it foolish?" They gently chided her and demanded an answer.

Loretta looked this way and that while longs strands of her blonde hair were blown to the corners of her mouth and held prisoner there. She smiled, blushed, and finally spoke.

"Sisters just don't tell their brothers that they like them." She was interrupted by more giggling and whispers.

"You are all terrible! None of *you* could tell your brother such a thing!" The entire group pretended innocence, and then they burst into laughter at the mere suggestion of even *liking* their own brothers.

What followed was a genuinely more serious discussion among the few older girls as to whether or not Loretta should share her feelings with her brother Sebastian. Some were adamant that she should tell him, but they admitted that they understood why she might decide she could not. At best, they agreed, it was awkward.

About this time, the woods grew ominously quiet. It was strange. Not a breath of air was on the move. The atmosphere became uncomfortably eerie. The young girls felt as if each of them had spoken their piece while an outsider had been eavesdropping, and they had been caught sharing their group's most private thoughts.

Then at once the atmosphere changed and filled with the sound of gasping young men as well as their footsteps – heavy footsteps! The boys were upon the boulders immediately, led by the colony's newest and evidently fastest boy. Oh, how Ed Buckmaster could run!

"What is it? What's the matter?" the girls demanded of the stampeding boys as they raced by the enormous, gray-green rocks. The young ladies were up and off the boulders quickly. The overwhelming excitement divested them of all their lady-like manners. Whatever had occurred was not to be observed by the boys alone!

"To the river! We've got to get to the river!" They were all trying to say so much that none of it seemed to make any sense at all. Their faces were wide-eyed and full of fright. The group zigzagged in and out of the trees, over fallen logs long dead and covered with moss, and onward to the river. Soon Loretta and the older girls were among the boys at a dead run until they found themselves struggling through the cane break near the river's edge. Dense growth made them all slow down, and voices were more easily understood.

Looking back over his shoulder in order to be heard above the shredding of the vegetation, and partially to impress the others, young Ed Buckmaster yelled to his followers, "I heard that someone drowned!"

He continued to hack through the burgundy and green branches in order to get to the riverbank first. The ground was muddy, but he did not seem to notice. To no one in particular he called out more news.

"I heard he was saving an old hound from the rapids!" yelled Eddie gasping for air as he slapped branches away from his face. "I think his name was Sebastian!"

SMALL TOWN TALE

Next came the incredulous screams of pedestrians. Some cries were full of fear while others were laden with anger...

LATE SPRING THROUGH EARLY AUTUMN they could be found most evenings sitting upon a comfortable park bench near the Trading Post on Main Avenue. A gaggle of friends, they enjoyed news, gossip, snacks, and humor. *Meetings* were not carved in stone, and attendance was voluntary. In no particular order, most evenings they would begin to gather after 6:30.

The group was a menagerie; a genuine cross section of Small Town America. Among them was a retired lino-type operator, a former limousine driver, the proprietor of Hawley's Trading Post, a souvenir shop appealing to tourists and locals alike, a retired mill owner, a handyman, and a retired teacher. Each had been a success in his or her field. They had become independent, raised families, formed long-lasting friendships, and quietly volunteered more than the average amount of community service. In a nutshell, they were decent folks.

Phi, nicknamed *The Chancellor* because like the head of a British University who represents his school, was the eldest and best represented his ring of friends with his wit. His arms and legs were thin, but he sported a modest paunch. A bespectacled man, he enjoyed wearing a cap that shaded his blue eyes and covered his gray hair. Having spent the last sixty years of his life running his print shop and publishing a local tri-weekly newspaper, by age seventy-seven Phil had become a walking-talking source of local history. Occasionally his friends teased, "Most of his reportage was accurate and true!"

The printer's attention to detail was impressive. He was the only member of their coterie who knew anything at all about the borough's one and only bank robbery which occurred during the 1960's. He was still able to recall and share such details as the getaway car's plate number as well as the make and model. Color? Nope. Phil was color blind. He could tell everyone how many were involved and how "… those banditos were dressed…", but ol' Phil could not differentiate between red shirts or green shirts. Color was the chink in his armor when it came to being a witness. If Phil announced he had seen a new, green Tesla ride by earlier in the day, long-time friends had to bet it was silver. There was no doubt what he saw was a Tesla, but unless listeners had known Phil a long time, the color was anyone's guess. Black was navy. Navy was forest green, and so it went.

Youngest of the group, Mark was fifty-five. Quiet by nature, this mountain of a man was a marvel when it came to general information such as local names, the gnarled branches of local family trees, and directions from here to there. He mastered entertainment trivia as well! Mark quoted lyrics of songs and poems, defined such terms as *rim shot* and knew the names of performers made famous for their various talents they shared with the world long before his time. He even knew Perry Como favored cashmere.

This quiet man's mammoth presence and salt-and-pepper, scruffy beard belied his more kind and gentle personality. More than once he appeared out of nowhere to assist each of his bench-loving comrades and others in the borough by lending a helpful hand. Thanks to the teacher in the group, Mark was assigned the moniker *Secretary of Defense* since he was the most physically imposing member of the group. Truth be told, it's likely he never confronted anyone in his life. So quiet was this man that if this local militia of six agreed to intentionally gather in the dark of night, five might question his presence among them.

Mark, too, was a car enthusiast. Chats among Phil, Mark, and Herb who was the team's *Secretary of Economics* were detailed, and such talks bubbled to the surface as vehicles passed by each evening. To them, spotting vanity plates was a sport, and there was never any pretense in an effort to impress each other. The three simply enjoyed a mutual respect as well as an appreciation of people and their automobiles.

The tallest of the group, Herb was a silver-haired, good-looking man with a complexion that hinted at a Mediterranean background. Rarely was he seen without a piece of candy in his mouth. For fun, he ambled up to the bench most evenings asking the same question pretending to sound sarcastic: "What's happening in the big city tonight?"

If seventy-six year old Herb had a tragic flaw, it was his endless pursuit to locate a better price someplace, hence his title. This gent reported where gasoline was cheapest and why bananas were a bad deal even at Wal Mart's low, low prices. "By tomorrow morning, the bananas I saw today will be good only for a banana bread recipe," he once uttered in disgust. To say the man was a tad critical at times is an understatement. Herb was the only person his friends knew who would find fault with the barrel of a shotgun pointed right at his chest by a mugger and disparage the mugger for improper care of his weapon. However, to be fair, he never found fault with his friends.

Bev was the seventy-five-year-old queen of the hive. Having lost Lou her wonderful husband of fifty years to illness, she was a widow. The bench crowd and the nightly meetings provided a degree of comfort, some much-needed fellowship, and the best medicine: humor.

Her Trading Post on Main Avenue with its large plate glass windows had an old-time charm. Her store invited visitors right off the sidewalk into its open arms where they discovered gifts and local treasures. Post cards and greeting cards lined its walls. For convenience to her everyday customers, daily newspapers were always available just inside her door. Those who enjoyed crafts found most necessary materials were in abundance at the back of the store upon several, wooden shelves. The scent of Yankee Candles permeated the entire store year around. And candies? No sweet tooth had a fighting chance. All of these charms awaited Bev's customers fewer than 100 feet from the shiny, burgundy park bench where she and her friends enjoyed the camaraderie of one another.

Bev was nicknamed "Rosey" the night she announced she had become the proverbial rose between two thorns. More than anything humor was the glue that bonded these individuals, and she certainly contributed her share.

When the gents paid attention to topics other than cars, she was able to hold her own. As much as any other in the group, she enjoyed hearing what was going on around the borough of Hawley and later sharing what she had learned during the hours in her store.

When not on the bench Bev was often perched upon her favorite chair in the front corner of her store. Sitting just out of the reach of the morning sun that cascaded through her windows, she greeted tourists and long-time friends alike. Cronies brought her news of anything they had heard was taking place in the county, while it was visitors to the borough who lined her purse and spoke of events taking place outside of the region.

Credible or not, stories Bev contributed to their evening discussions were some of the most interesting since her Trading Post introduced her to people from all walks of life. As he listened Satchel often thought that if she sat still long enough the world came to Bev through her burgundy Trading Post door that framed a beautiful pane of glass which she kept sparkling clean.

Their queen was dubbed *Secretary of Animal Affairs.* Kind to all animals, she rescued many a kitten over the years and regularly fed treats to any dog on a leash when it passed by the store's front door. Two pups in particular were regulars; one a gray Chihuahua and the other a black and brown Rottweiler. They automatically halted at her door each day, refusing to proceed until Bev came out to reward them for their loyalty.

None of the six friends was a true Hawley native, and Butch had lived in Hawley for the shortest time. Once a limousine driver, life dealt him a cruel blow that cost him both of his legs just above his knees. Thanks to his courage and friendly demeanor, "the guy in the wheel chair wearing a cowboy hat" grew to know everyone as he quietly motored around Hawley, and they grew to know him. When someone else might have cried, "Woe is me!" Butch offered a large smile and robustly greeted others with, "Good morning! How are you?", and he genuinely listened.

Butch parked his motorized chair alongside of Mark during the many evenings when he was present. Perhaps his friend's size made him feel safe, or maybe he parked there since they were both excellent listeners.

Smacking of humor and a touch of irony, Butch was their *Secretary of Transportation.* In reality, none of the titles meant anything, but Butch enjoyed his as much as anyone. Some nights he brought details to their get together and filled a great deal of gaps in local gossip. His details were occasionally surprising.

Sitting at the base of a forested river valley, Hawley developed into a relatively flat community. Some roads out of the borough cut through its surrounding hills, and a couple of them were quite steep. However, none were a problem for Butch, sidewalks or no sidewalks. There were evenings when his banter revealed he had visited some of Hawley's more elevated locations.

Never thinking of himself as handicapped, he found great pleasure in the freedom and stealth his chair afforded him. He enjoyed traversing the borough and startled many in some of the places they spotted him.

Even the ordinarily stoic Mark raised his eyebrows when Butch reported the annual return of the osprey to its perch alongside the lake's scenic overlook above Hawley.

"Who told you that?" the handy man inquired.

"Told me? Nobody told me. I saw them." Having gained everyone's ear with his gravelly voice, Butch explained his ability to transcend at least some of his handicap. "When the weather's nice, I buzz up once a week."

Despite the size of the task, neither Mark nor any of the group questioned the veracity of his report. Mark never even blinked. All he did was look out over Main Avenue's classical store fronts and softly announce, "I wish I had seen it."

When events of interest took place, it was noted by members and eventually shared with the others. Nothing was off the table. Evening's golden hue upon each of the turn-of-the-century buildings added to the newly painted store fronts, and the scene was later reported. Cloud formations, some of them pink against blue sky, were a favorite to discuss. There were evenings when near-accidents, U-turns, and the absence of bar room regulars were small stories, but they were valuable fodder for discussion nonetheless. And when one of Hawley's local gendarmes rode by and was spotted texting? Oh my! That earned a headline for sure.

Occasionally there was a blood drive held in the basement of any of the many local churches. Although each had donated over the years, few had given blood as often as Phil, Mark, and Butch. One evening they spoke of blood types while sharing the little bit they knew on the topic. Butch surprised them once again.

They listened to his scratchy voice as he spoke. "If you have Type O negative blood, the good news is, anyone else can use it. You are the *universal donor.*"

Then Butch took a drag on his cigarette and continued. "The down side of it is, and it's a rather *big* downside, anyone who is a Type O negative can only accept blood from another Type O negative donor. It's somewhat of a bummer."

Perhaps for emphasis, he snuffed out his smoke before he added, "To make matters a bit worse, Type O negative blood is not common."

Bev leaned forward, looked down the bench and asked what the others were wondering. "How did you learn so much about blood?"

"Guess who is O negative," Butch replied.

"That explains your beard," Phil added in an attempt to lighten the mood.

Mark just stared at his friend sitting to his right. As always he was listening, but he had the look of a man who might want to speak, but he abstained from doing so.

Natural cycles were a favorite topic of discussion, especially the regularity of one blue heron that passed them by each night at nearly the same time. As autumn approached and daylight waned earlier, its flight was taking place earlier as well. Headed up Middle Creek above the Main Avenue Bridge, it loped along as if it was taking its time and making observations all its own

Someone joked, "Maybe it looks at us and notices we're still here." The enjoyment of seeing the heron was doubled one evening when a second such bird passed above the cement bridge as well.

"Must be poker night up the creek."

"No, that's his girlfriend."

The Secretary of Transportation earned a chuckle with, "Mr. Blue? A girl friend? No. He's had one fish too many and arranged for a designated flyer."

These meetings went on for years from May through early October. During all this time, the patterns of certain locals evolved, and also were duly noted. Point of fact, Bev was involved in one such daily ritual. Each afternoon about 5:30, she locked her store's entrance and shuffled along slowly to the diner half a block up Main Ave. Her stride was seemingly an uncomfortable one, but she hiked along and usually met John and Cathy for dinner in the same booth. By her dinner's end, the bench crowd had already begun to gather. When they observed her return, they knew it was nearly 7:00 p.m. Such was "Rosey's ritual" as it came to be known.

Similarly, there was an area motorcyclist who rode by at nearly the same time each evening, and she didn't go unnoticed. With long blonde hair and wearing black from helmet to boots, what made her stand out was that she rode the quietest Harley Davidson any of them had ever witnessed. It, too, was flat black accented with a modest amount of chrome.

"Must be a ninja..."

"...or a Johnny Cash fan," Phil quietly added. That's all that was ever spoken. They moved on to subsequent observations seamlessly, but the cyclist had made their list.

A time came when she failed to ride by a few nights in a row. As if concerned, it was Herb who pointed out that the biker actually not been seen in a few days. "I hope she's okay," Herb uttered sincerely.

"Maybe she's just working late."

"Maybe she was wearing pink, and we never noticed her," Phil teased. He *knew* what would follow.

"How would you know?" was their simultaneous reaction.

"Maybe the bridge was up," was the quip of the night and resulted in a group guffaw, for everyone knew the bridge was incapable of moving up or down. Laughter was the poultice that kept them coming back; 'twas their drug of choice.

Warmer seasons passed. Winters came and went. Throughout colder times the troupe just stopped showing up. No one announced, "This is it for the year" or something as official as "Tonight's the last meeting. See you in the spring." Attendance abated naturally. Inches and then feet of wet, heavy snow, a coating of slick ice, or just total darkness assumed their place 'til spring.

Like the robins that quietly and almost suddenly disappeared from everyone's radar with no fanfare until their return the following spring, Phil, Herb, and all the others just disappeared from the bench. From time to time they would see each other in a market, but they saw one another far less regularly. Never were they seen lingering upon what became a cold, metal park bench; albeit the very same shiny, burgundy bench that was so wonderfully comfortable in warmer weather.

Regulars who drove by nightly might have noticed their disappearance just as birders note migrations. Perhaps commuters thought, "It's only mid-October, and they're gone already. It's going to be a long winter," but then again maybe no one noticed at all.

This cycle of friendship moved into its ninth year, and little things changed while bigger, more well-established things remained the same. Glenn's music store and his lessons right across the street from where they sat were a continued success. Pat's Bar? No one could recall a time when it *did not* exist. Hawley's one and only travel agency, on the other hand, "Went back to the city on the bus."

Satchel the retired teacher once surveyed, "Does anyone like the new banners upon our street lights?" Small by design and shaped like pennants, they were meant to welcome tourists.

As only Herb could, he replied, "The Council could've purchased larger ones in bolder colors for nearly the same price." His counterparts wondered aloud how he came to such a conclusion, so he told them. "I was in the business. Remember?"

A fresh, new spring season had begun. The troupe had returned, and it was back in stride. If they were ever to share a mantra, if the six of them were buried side by side, no one would have been surprised if their headstones were engraved with, "Slow and steady wins the race." Six words. Six people. Six friends. Six historical markers.

They never missed a beat and picked up right where they left off the previous autumn. All was as it should be until the tragic day when Butch cruised into the crosswalk connecting both sides of Main Avenue. He was nearly in the middle the diner's intersection just 150 feet from his friends on the bench.

Over the years, each of them was disgusted by impatient drivers, and on one evening in particular they witnessed the actions of a young man who would change their lives forever. Music blaring from his Jeep, he pulled up second in line just short of the intersection of Keystone and Main. He cared not one iota about what stopped the muddy, green pickup in front of him. He didn't look ahead to see that the pickup's driver was providing safe passage for Butch, but instead he chose to whip his canvas-topped, golden Jeep over Main Avenue's double yellow line and pass. What followed was a loud thump, the crunching of metal, and Butch's painful shrieks.

Next came the incredulous screams of pedestrians. Some cries were full of fear while others were laden with anger, for what barely preceded their shouting was the squealing of tires as the Jeep sped away, for its driver had no intention of stopping. Having been propelled from his chair into the air, Butch landed solidly upon the blacktop road surface and rolled. Consequently, he was nearly run over a second time!

Having witnessed this from the group's vantage point, Bev began to scream in disbelief. The spinning rubber tires smoked and continued their sick song as the runaway driver passed them by and accelerated. Adding to the brief and bizarre atmosphere of the moment, loud music still blared as it quickly raced by the witnesses on their way to Butch's aid.

Not Mark. He was headed in the opposite direction toward his old Chevy Blazer parked around the corner on River Street. While the others were thinking First Aid, he was thinking of capture.

Once it was out of sight and had passed the Post Office, the direction the Jeep traveled was anyone's guess. Mark figured the driver could drive faster if he stayed upon the main drag. He also realized that there were three immediate turns off the highway that might offer unlimited back roads where the speeding Jeep might have raced unseen.

Initially he felt the driver might prefer a hiding spot to a speedy attempt at escape. Mark felt that at some point the driver who had hit and perhaps killed his friend Butch would have to take a moment to slow down and collect his thoughts. Such introspection was not something a hit-and-run driver would do along a highway in full view of many others who might be looking for him; people like Mark who wanted to wring his neck.

Mark grasped his steering wheel tightly...white-knuckles tight. Which turnoff might he have taken? Up Columbus Avenue by the Post Office, a narrow road that gradually rose out of the valley? Straight uphill on Spruce Street towards what eventually became a rough, tree-lined dirt road? Or a sharper right-hand turn out of Hawley that led to even more flat, yet winding roads?

⊰≣≣⊱

Bev was a wreck and stood toward the back of the crowd that gathered in the middle of the intersection. Phil was uneasy as well, but being the borough's former Fire Chief he had become inured to such scenes, having seen more than his share of ugly accidents. Kneeling at Butch's side, he did what he felt he should do to provide Butch some comfort and a modicum of dignity. The ex-chief covered the poor man's bloody, shredded scalp with his own long-sleeved outer shirt. Butch was taking on an ashen appearance, and the EMT's did not arrive quickly enough to suit his friends.

"Herb, before I forget!" Phil suddenly called out over his shoulder as he comforted Butch the best he knew how. "Take out your pen and write this down." Phil knew his old friend always had a pen and pocket tablet with him, and Herb was quick to react.

"Go ahead. Shoot!" Long-time friends, Herb already knew what Phil was doing.

"2007 Jeep Wrangler. NJ plates…and you're not going to believe this part…he has a vanity plate: 'CATCHME'."

Herb stared in disbelief. "You're kidding." Then he asked, "What color?" Immediately he remembered to whom he was speaking. "Never mind."

Still in touch with 911, Satchel used his Crime Watch training to gather information and share what he could with the Call Center. Herb showed him the information on his tablet, and it was passed along immediately. It frustrated him greatly that he had no hint as to what direction the hit and run driver had chosen to escape. Like most everyone else, he had been focused on Butch.

"Where's Mark?" he asked Herb. "Maybe he saw him take off."

"Is Mark the big fella?" a bystander asked. "Scraggly beard…baseball cap…sleeveless sweatshirt?"

Still on the phone with the Call Center, the professor nodded vigorously and said to the elderly stranger, "Yes, he's the one. Have you seen him?"

"Uh yeah. Kind of hard to miss." The gent pointed at Main Avenue as he added, "He ran down the middle of this street right after the accident." The man pointed in the direction of River Street. "He hopped in a big, ol' truck and took off after the guy. I think."

"Phil!"

The former fire chief's high-pitched voice came out of the crowd. "What?"

"Any chance at all that you know Mark's plate number?"

To the surprise of many at the scene, Phil rattled it off, and the information was passed along. Satchel's final words to the Call Center operator were a warning. "If you see that Blazer anyplace near that Jeep, you'd better call the coroner. Mark and Butch are good friends." Then he stopped the call.

Bev took Herb's arm. After some deep breaths, she decided she had to go to Butch's side. "Phil, is he conscious?" she asked in her high-pitched voice.

She was worrisome, and what she really wanted to learn was whether or not their friend was still alive but could not bring herself to say the words. Arriving at the front of the crowd, she whimpered, "Oooh, Butch. Look at you. Poor Butch." She turned to Herb and started to sob. Gentleman that he was he gently led her away, for he understood she had seen all she could handle.

Upon the seeing the ambulance pull up at the intersection, the gathering moved aside. In reality, their arrival had taken but a few minutes. Curious witnesses began to gawk as Phil told paramedics what he knew, and then he retreated and indicated that onlookers should do the same.

Butch heard nothing it seemed. Hopefully he felt nothing more as well. Phil glanced at his outer shirt as he entered his second-floor apartment and saw a lot of blood. "O negative," he thought to himself. "Was it just yesterday we shared that discussion?"

To the folks all around, the ambulance driver asked, "Does he have family?"

Herb stepped from the curb and replied, "Not around here. His daughter works at night, but I don't know exactly where she might be."

Satchel felt bad having to admit what Herb said was true. They just did not know. To himself he wondered, "How could we be friends and not know such details?" As the driver turned away the professor asked, "Do you need anyone to ride along with him?"

"No, but you're welcome to meet us at the ER. You might be of help with registration."

The ambulance was underway with its siren blaring. Quickly the fire company volunteers were able to clean the intersection once the police finished a thorough investigation. So efficient were they that only the Jeep's skid marks were left behind. Just as quickly, onlookers quietly moved on. Some were still visibly shaken.

A few minutes passed after he cleaned himself, and the Chancellor returned to the sidewalk in front of his print shop. His sole intention was to check on Bev. With Herb, he shared his suspicions about Mark.

"I think he went after the guy. As much as I want the jerk caught, I hope it's not Mark who catches him."

Bev looked up at the two of them. Already diminutive, this event appeared to have made her smaller. "Do you think Mark would hurt him, Phil?"

"If he does," replied the worried ex-Chief, "I wouldn't blame him, but it would get him into a lot of trouble." He looked around and spotted the remaining member of their group. "What's the professor doing?"

"He's looking for his cell phone."

In all the excitement, his cell phone had indeed been misplaced. Before Satchel took off for Honesdale's hospital, he decided to first look around for it a while. Finding his phone was not as important as Butch's well-being, but at the same time he did not want to go through replacing his cell phone all over again, for not long ago it had been stolen. That event caused enough hassle.

After a moment, the others announced they would search for it, thus freeing him to depart for the hospital ten miles up the road. As they watched him drive off to the hospital, Herb thought he remembered that only moments before the terrible accident Mark had borrowed the missing phone. It was memorable in that Mark never desired to own such a phone. He had made that abundantly clear.

"I don't want anyone bothering me with calls," he told them all in what Bev called his *tough-guy* voice. While searching from bench to intersection, they agreed it was odd that Mark had need for a cell phone just before the tragedy befell his friend. They also agreed that given the circumstances it was an easy enough fact to overlook.

Then the tall, tanned seventy-six year old had another idea. "Let's dial the number. Maybe Mark will answer."

⚞⚟

It took but a few seconds for Mark to choose the highway. He figured it afforded any driver the opportunity to cover the most ground. It would let a hit-and-run driver put more distance between himself and his crime. The decision proved to be a fortuitous one, for as Fate would have it, the golden-toned music machine was running low on gas.

"Are you kidding me?" he angrily whispered to himself as he pulled in the Sunoco Express Mart to the right of the highway. In micro seconds, Mark realized there were several things he had not considered as he was tracking the Jeep. "How big is this guy? What if he was armed? Would he put up much of a fight?" Most important of all, "What will I do with him when I confront him and capture him?"

Mark initiated his spontaneous plan of action when he pulled up closely adjacent to the Jeep in order to prevent any access to the driver's side and steering wheel. Inches separated the two vehicles. When the runaway driver saw what Mark had done and watched him exit his Blazer, he feared trouble.

Mark's concerns of a moment ago? They rapidly flew out his driver's-side window. His bearded face did nothing to hide his anger as he approached his prey. The image of his friend's body in flight was burned into his psyche, and with each step forward more adrenaline pumped throughout his body. His mission was to avenge what he had witnessed.

Intimidated by his adversary's sheer size and demeanor, the owner of the Jeep made no attempt to escape what he thought was inevitable. He opted to simply put up his hands in front of his chest as an indication of surrender. In seconds, Mark captured both of his wrists and tightened his vice-like grip.

At that very moment, from deep in his rear jeans pocket, a cell phone was heard ringing. It was a first for Mark, and it confirmed what he had said all along: "I don't want anybody bothering me with calls."

Briefly it was considered whether or not the call would provide information regarding Butch's condition. Mark even considered whether or not there was a risk in releasing one of the wrists of the man he held tightly in front of him. He decided to ignore the call and forced his prey to his knees.

As if on cue, a second alarm was heard in the distance. It was the ambulance's siren becoming increasingly easier to hear. They could tell it was speeding toward them and the hospital three miles up the highway. Already uncomfortably loud, the sirens became cacophonous as the orange and white vehicle screamed by the Express Mart and just as quickly began to subside in the distance, until finally fading into welcome silence.

"Mister," he growled in his most minatory voice at the young man kneeling below him adjacent to the pump's hose still dangling from the Jeep's tank, "you better pray the passenger in that ambulance is alive." Then he added in a tone more threatening than his first, "And you better hope he *stays* alive."

Mark had missed the phenomenon of the gathering onlookers back in Hawley, but he quickly realized he was the center of attention in the market's parking lot. "Call 911!" he shouted gruffly to no one in particular. "The cops are going to want to know this fella's whereabouts!" The manager of the market did as he was told.

Avoiding eye contact, Mark noticed dog tags around the neck of his prisoner. Releasing one wrist, Mark reached down to grab the small, shiny metal plates. Once they were in his grasp, he yanked at their chain with as much strength as he could to remove them from his captive's neck. The chain shattered into pieces, but Mark had what he wanted right in the palm of his calloused hand.

He stared at the tags intently, for he wanted to know just who this silent man was still kneeling before him. Over the noise of the police pulling into the mart, and in a voice that indicated surprise and disbelief, Mark was heard to ask, "You're in the Army?"

The man nervously nodded his affirmation.

"Well, Soldier," Mark growled, "I know that it ain't the dog tags' purpose, but your tags just now saved your life."

"What do you mean?" the soldier asked in a shaken voice as the police rushed in their direction.

Standing tall above the man, with loud voices in the air all around them, Mark struggled with replying. For a brief moment, he experienced a new desire: hurting someone. Better judgment prevailed.

"These metal tags of yours indicate your blood type is O negative."

SEE THINGS MY WAY

—❧❦—

"You're no different! You're another prankster.
You're a punk." Gus DeGrig would have loved
to stomp around in anger, but from experience
he knew that would only make things worse.

ALL THE YEARS OF WAKING up in darkness had hardened him.
He became bitter and unfriendly. He had become a loner.
For years, family members tried their best to keep him active,
tried to show him his life could still have meaning and be
enjoyed. He could be productive despite his blindness.
Eventually they all gave up.

Deep inside he knew he had only himself to blame for
his handicap. A simple precaution, protective goggles, were
all that stood between an everyday occurrence and a tragic
accident. During the days, weeks, and months after he was
blinded, no one spoke to him about it openly, and his hardened façade rejected any thought of counseling. Rarely was

the accident discussed. Maybe if someone had mentioned it things might have been different. Maybe.

Gus DeGrig lost his sight at the mill where he worked when he was thirty. Fifteen years had come and gone since that day. During that time, he lost his wife, he lost his family, and he lost his friends. They had not abandoned him; he had driven them away. Gus had been alone long enough to have thought about his indiscretion, yet over the years he continued to blame everyone else. He was not yet man enough to admit that what had happened to him was no one's fault but his own.

As people without sight can do, he learned to compensate for his handicap with his remaining senses. During those odd moments when toast would burn or milk was left out to sour, Gus was glad he had his sense of smell. Salty pretzels delivered to him and left upon his porch with the rest of his groceries never tasted so delicious with a glass of cold beer. There was a night when his sense of touch might have saved his life. He knew something was amiss when he grasped the metal knob upon his basement door, and it was terribly hot. He nearly burned down his home by unwittingly letting a cigar ash fall into his basement garbage as he listened to his dehumidifier, a weekly routine he felt was important. The machine usually ran quietly and kept his storage area from smelling musty. Gus stopped smoking that night.

Many things happened over those troublesome years. Events transformed him from Mr. DeGrig who worked in the mill into that "old man". It was what the neighborhood kids called him from a safe distance when they rode their bikes down the hill in front of his house as he sat on his porch upon a rocking chair behind the gray railing's white spindles. He was old, and he was only forty-five.

The neighborhood was abundant with kids. Usually they stayed clear. However, there came a day that was different. Those soft footsteps Gus heard coming up his unpainted, wooden plank steps were not made by an adult, and he knew it.

"Too light even for a delicate woman," DeGrig observed from his favorite chair just inside his screen door where he often listened to his radio talk shows. He knew from years of experience that the top three steps creaked easily under the weight of any adult. He sat listening intently.

"Who's there?" cried out a loud, gruff voice from behind the storm door. His stern inquiry started the eleven-year-old boy who dared to approach his residence and stand upon his porch. Suddenly all was quiet. A breeze could be heard teasing the wind chimes out on the porch.

After several ticks of the octagon clock on the wall, the boy summoned his courage and introduced himself through the screen. "My name is Gustave...Gus Smoot." They were words spoken timidly, but they successfully drifted through the darkened screen door.

DeGrig quickly evaluated the lad based upon the unsteady tone of his soft voice. Visitors at the man's door were infrequent, and in his cranky, adult mind he sensed young Gustave's voice oozed uncertainty. Perhaps he was intimidated and scared.

The grumpy recluse aimed to keep an upper hand, so he continued his gruffness, but he was not as loud the second time. "Son, it's unusual that a kid sets foot on my doorstep. What is it you want?" Then he added, "Let me guess."

Getting up from his favorite chair he approached the door to the porch. DeGrig noted that young Gustave remained very still. Perhaps he was ready to run. In order to scare the boy, the man yelled, "You're selling something!"

Startled Gustave jumped back in retreat. Despite what others had told him he was still surprised by the older man's harshness and volume. Then he remembered our advice: "Be patient with the man. Give him a chance."

"Well, kid?" DeGrig continued when there was no reply.

"My name is..."

"Yeah, yeah. Sure. Gustave...Gus Smoot." Degrig tried again to intimidate the boy. "You already told me that, and with a name like that I wouldn't repeat it too often." There was a pause, and he added, "I bet kids at school have a field day with that name of yours." He thought he would badger this kid, and he would scoot like the others.

"Strange you should say that," young Gus countered. "Our names are the same." Then quickly before DeGrig could interrupt him, young Gus added, "My name is Gus just like yours." The eleven-year-old visitor had scored at least a momentary victory during their exchange. It was uncomfortable for the older Gus. He did not like it one bit.

"Just tell me what you want, kid," insisted the elder angrily.

47

"May I come in?" The lad felt for the screen door handle, anticipating a "Yes" from DeGrig. The door opened, and soon he was seated. From his quiet movements, Gus DeGrig was reminded that this young boy was slight of stature, yet the kid had guts. He was not at all puerile by nature. Briefly he wondered about the kid's age when he realized where the boy had seated himself.

Shifting gears mentally he barked, "Hey, don't sit there! I sit there!" On his own turf, the man felt imperious, the exact reason why he was rarely seen outside his home or off his own property.

Moving quickly, young Gustave fumbled for yet another seat. Then it all happened: the nudge at the tip of his cane and the silent anticipation of a crash. The young boy had accidentally broken a fragile figurine that was a fisherman, once a gift from DeGrig's wife. Entering a building for the first time was an unsettling experience for any blind person. Feeling terrible for what he had just done, compounded by Mr. Degrig's rough demeanor, Gustave's heart pounded in his chest. He knew not what to expect.

"Geez, kid, what did you do?" the man yelled explosively. Anyone on the street outside would have heard him.

"I'm sorry!" Gustave replied in earnest. "I couldn't see it!" There was beautiful sincerity in his tone, but the old Gus did not recognize it.

"Listen! Don't be a wise guy." Furious, DeGrig stood still. If he could have, he would have been seeing red at that moment. "I'm blind, and you rub my face in it."

"Mr. De-"

"You're no different! You're another prankster. You're a punk." Gus DeGrig would have loved to stomp around in anger, but from experience he knew that would only make things worse. There is no room for unnecessary motion in the lifestyle of a blind person, especially indoors. The loss of one's sense of direction might not only lead to injury, but death as well.

"Mr. DeGrig!" the boy interjected. He had finally suffered enough torment and screamed, "I am blind, too!"

There's no doubt that everyone in the neighborhood could have heard this ballistic conversation and felt its result. Screen doors on a summer day have a way of letting out even the most subtle arguments. This confrontation had gone nuclear for a moment. However, a young boy by the funny name of Gustave Smoot had finally penetrated that shell that for years could not be penetrated. For the first time in years, Gus Degrig sat down quietly and in a different chair.

"You're blind?" His words were spoken softly.

"Uh huh," Gustave replied nervously. Tears streamed down his soft, puffy face. "I've been blind all my life. I was born blind." He was still standing in a room he knew not.

Not used to feeling the way he was feeling, DeGrig waited a moment to gather his thoughts. Finally, he spoke. "Why didn't you say you are blind when you came up my steps... stood outside my door?"

"Being blind doesn't usually enter my mind. I guess I can't make a big deal out of something I never had."

Older Gus mellowed even more when he heard, "I thought maybe we could share our stories and maybe become friends. Everybody needs friends."

"There was a time when I *could* see," mumbled the man. That old, familiar tightness was returning to the surface of his mind.

"I know."

"You knew?" Younger Gus could sense the surprise in Mr. DeGrig's voice.

My mom and dad explained what happened to you a long time ago." In terms an eleven year old could share, Gustave Smoot went on to explain how his mom and I had known Gus DeGrig and observed his metamorphosis from afar. In a kind way, little Gus said his parents had felt sorry for this man. "I guess you could say I learned from your mistakes." Then he added, "I hope you don't mind me saying that."

That old tightness came and went...evaporated quickly. Mr. DeGrig continued to speak in softer tones. "Go on, Gus." He even found that he liked having a friend with the same name as his. It felt right.

"It's just that I don't want to grow up without friends. My parents kind of understand your feelings, but I think you let it trouble you too much." Young Gustave turned, tapped, and started for the door. Things were quiet outside, quiet enough that the Graff family's hound could be heard in the distance.

For the first time, DeGrig noticed that tapping of Gustave's cane. "Where are you going?" the elder asked the boy.

"I've got to go. My folks will wonder where I am." Then in words that belied his youth, "I'm sure they're wondering how all of this has worked out."

"Are you able to use a phone? Can you call them?" For the very first time in years, Old Man DeGrig had invited someone to stay and visit.

"Sure. I think they would like that. I know I will."

My wife answered the phone, spoke to our son and told him to stay. I watched her gently hang up the phone with trembling fingers. She cried for an hour.

GENERATIONS

❧

The hunters worked quickly but carefully.
They knew not if cremating one of their own
would draw the beast in their direction...

KELCHI PLAYED IN THE FOREST of the Keshishian Valley not far from a slate-colored sea. Taller than most his age, he was the son of older parents who were greatly respected among their clansmen. From Tiko and Lavella, Kelchi learned early that respect was important, so he maneuvered quietly among his people whenever dragging firewood back to his family's lodge, a chore not uncommon for children his age. He minded his business and drew no attention to himself.

When their duties were fulfilled the children of Keshishia enjoyed a day full of play. Kelchi and other girls and boys enjoyed pretending they were their ancestors, the brave hunters and explorers the village storytellers exalted. Imaginary hunts were an important part of their culture since hunting and fishing provided game to support a lifestyle so dependent upon its environment. The valley was lush; surrounded by the tallest of trees. Many firmly rooted themselves adjacent to the mountains and cliffs not too distant from either bank along the generous river.

More than half of the Keshishian people lived along the Miranda or "Wandering River", so named for its serpentine course. Having paddled their dugouts each spring over great distances toward the sea, villagers believed the moniker to be appropriate for this great and winding waterway. Having sustained Keshishians since the clan settled in the valley 100 years earlier, the river was shown respect in the villagers' rituals, their songs, and their legends. Unlike most children his age, Kelchi memorized each and every one.

Favorite legends revealed in detail how their organic lifestyle was not without a history, interruptions, and responsibilities. According to the fireside tale weavers, the clan was formed by Kelchi's great-great grandfather Dalin, and Keshishians were comprised of an entire people believing their origin traced back to the Keshishian Valley, hence the name of their clan.

Some stories were humorous and light-hearted, meant to bring joy and comfort to the community. By design, others taught lessons creatively. A favorite was a tale that celebrated the yearly cycle of the seasons. It told of long winter naps and the magic of the waking seeds each spring. Young ones learned that when nurtured these gifts of nature would thrive throughout summer and share their fruits to be harvested each fall. A successful cycle was the result of clans-men working together responsibly and being rewarded with new seeds to be properly stored in their lodgings until the following spring.

Lessons instilled the importance of sharing the work necessary to prepare for Keshishia's long winters. Even the youngest around the fires knew that winter brought with it difficulties and dangers, so successful preparation was of tre-mendous importance.

"Even the smallest squirrel scurries about collecting food for his family," Tonkin the Teller reminded them. "And when all the squirrels do the same, all of them benefit." Tonkin fed upon the interest of those wide-eyed children as well as the expressions upon their golden-brown faces he watched by the light of the flames dancing in front of them. "Be obser-vant throughout the day, and watch what the animals do. Learn from them as well as your elders."

The oldest verses sadly spun a tale of Keshishian men and women who, no matter how brave, were unable to defeat a winged monster that plagued the clan for generations. As he grew older and listened more intently, Kelchi under-stood that even his own father Tiko held a respectful awe for the tales regarding a terrifying, flying monster his peopled named the Glazier. Oh, the horrible things it had done!

Memories of battling with the Glazier instilled honor among the villagers, reinforcing the belief that honor must always be maintained. Never did they search for a new home or run in fear of the beast. Despite understanding how it had attacked them after their arrival and suspecting it would attack unexpectedly again one day, the terror it caused was still not enough to drive them away. To all Keshishians, the beast was a test of their courage.

When Kelchi was twelve, autumn arrived with more than just colors and seasonal change. With it a came a new tale of courage. Few were the nights when Counsel decreed a new saga was to become part of their traditional lore; a fresh final fall song that had to be sung. The moment was not lost upon him.

Tellers awaited a night when the moon painted shadows with its milky, blue light. When but dying embers of their fire remained, not one single clansman rose to miss a refrain. The tale glorified the courage of twenty clansmen led by Tiko, this proud twelve-year-old's father. Verse after verse described their actions, and how they united to fight the cruel Glazier on their own terms. It mattered not that its origin was recent; only that the tale was to be remembered as "The Greatest Keshishian Legend" ever told, passed around campfires throughout the river valley for all generations to come. The following is that legend.

⚔

According to Keshishian lore, Dalin was the head of their clan. Kelchi's great, great grandfather was strong like a bull, wore reddish hair to his shoulders and grew a full beard to match. Men dared not question his wisdom and leadership, for none could argue his judgment. Along with Jacar, his stocky, imposing figure of a son, the two formed a brave and curious duo. Together these men desired to discover what lie over the distant horizons surrounding the land of their own forefathers who made them a people of the plains.

Courageously they left behind some of their family, many friends, and also their homes to traverse the all-too-familiar grassy plains in search of what was to be discovered in the distance. These men did not travel alone, as several cousins shared their desire and followed their lead. In total, there were fifteen future Kashishians on the move. Each was required to walk aside pack animals which were greatly-appreciated gifts from those they left behind.

The explorers lived off game that had always been plentiful and at times was discovered to be dangerous, though as a rule, most animals on the plains were not a great challenge or threat. Armed with bows, these brave explorers easily provided for their families. There were, however, occasions when hunters for the small group found themselves in peril.

The undulating prairie grew summer grasses to the height of a full-sized man, and it swayed gently in the wind in various locales. Leopards stalked their prey among these seemingly harmless waves of greenish brown and relied on stealth as much as their raw power. The tall grass was a perfect cover. More than once Jacar and his father met hungry panthers face to face, only to return to camp victorious after deadly battles. Time passed, wounds healed, and the troupe moved on toward their target: the mysterious green mountains looming impressively large in the distance.

By the dry, hot summer's end, lightning strikes, too, were a threat. Grasses were tinder for the massive bolts which crackled daily before dark at the end of a hot, humid day. Blazing flames grew as fires were fanned by the hot winds all fires create. Escaping the blazing purge, the travelers were happy to look to the distant mountains, travel in their direction, and leave the charred plains behind.

The day finally came when they conquered the mountains for which they longed by snaking through lush defiles among the rocks and cliffs hidden behind the tallest of trees. Dalin challenged his clansmen to fight the urge to stop until they had searched the banks of the river that flowed on ahead. At long last, adhering to the bold leader's wish, they discovered a valley they knew could be their new home.

Yet nothing they experienced during their journey had prepared them for what was to follow. Two moons after settling along the River Miranda the Glazier first attacked the valley's newest inhabitants. 'Twas fortuitous no victims were crushed by its talons that night, and the quick-growing clan was ever on the alert forevermore. Those who followed to become part of their community were warned of the beast's existence.

Time passed. Fall and winter were survived. This was a hardy, new clan indeed. The first babies of the Keshishian people were born, and among them was a lad who came to be known as Elijah, son of Jacar who would one day cradle his grandson Kelchi in his powerful arms.

The second attack upon the Dalin's original Keshishians occurred many years after the first. Elijah was but a child. The great, winged monster arrived during a storm, surprising the village despite the sentries it placed in strategic positions. From their mountain vantage points, the plan was to see, hear or feel the monster's approach long before it would get close to the valley below. It was hoped the sentries would have ample time to warn everyone with the ringing of the village's iron bells which had been built along the mountains surrounding their village far below.

As fate would have it, the monster awakened at night. The winds were wicked, and clouds raced through the sky obscuring any sound or sight of the monster's movement. Making things worse, the monster flew toward Keshishia with the wind in its face. Any noise it might have made was incapable of ever being heard. The smells from Keshishian cook fires helped it find the village's gentle people. It was as if they were inviting trouble, they never stood a chance.

The first to fall prey to the appetite of the monster were the northernmost sentries. Not one shriek was heard by the remaining sentries or villagers alike. The wild winds that night prevented that. As a result, the bells of Keshishia were never sounded. Branches cracked, trees uprooted, and there were repeated brilliant flashes of lightning followed by cacophonous claps of thunder, the sounds of which were unmatched by any thing of earth. Surely it was a night made for a monster's attack.

Next to die were the poor villagers who were easily caught off guard. It wasn't that they were asleep. No one could sleep on such a night. Legend has it that on this night only the young survived, and even some of them didn't make it into the shelters or the forest sanctuary. Hardly able to run, the elders of Keshishia were easy prey in the open areas between their thatched houses and their hideouts. It was told that even their horrible screams were never heard above the thunder or the terrible screeching of the giant, bird-like creature.

Those who survived that nightmarish attack hoped and prayed that their descendants would never suffer a similar fate. They considered moving their Keshishian culture to lands yet unknown; moving while the monster slept on its belly filled with their loved ones. But being an honorable people they could not bring themselves to do so, for they knew that clans further down the shoreline would suffer the exact same fate. Keshishians believed the monster was their problem, not that of their neighbors to the south. To them there was no honor in escape, but that honor could be realized only in victory over the beast.

The clan regrouped and defense planning continued. Kelchi's great grandfather Jacar was one of the survivors during the dreadful night of the second attack. His family had prepared better than some. Given the choice to build near the river at the center of Keshishia and along its shoreline where everyone loved to be, Jacar's father Dalin prudently advised a more remote location be chosen, one closer to the forest and the protection its ancient and colossal trees afforded his family. The decision was prudent, having saved their lives including Elijah's.

When not toting kindling from the woods or not out at play along the river, Elijah would quietly place himself among his village elders. He listened to the stories of the horrible monster that ravaged his village the year before his birth; how its talons would shred not only the flesh of its victims, but the metal of armed guards as well.

Keshishia was a region the creature attacked with no regularity or pattern. Yet when it did attack, its wrath was unmatched by any other natural force its victims could fathom. Why, in the shadows of this phenomenal and seemingly eventual peril, did the villagers choose not to move? Why had they not uprooted themselves generations ago? Only for honor?

At long last, years passed on and there were no further attacks. Conversations of honor abated. Still Kelchi's great-grandfather and those of his generation passed along stories of the Glazier in the hope that someday it would be defeated.

More days than not, mornings were begun with beautiful sunrises. Divided by its river, and located near the mountain base which was believed to be the home of their deity, Keshishia was surrounded by forest greens everywhere. The golden light of the morning sun painted everything in the bright new colors of day. Mists along the great banks of the river sparkled in the morning sun until they vaporized and gradually disappeared. It was said that each drop of mist was the soul of each victim longing to revisit his home. So great was the village's beauty.

The river Miranda meandered down from above, dividing the village into two parts as fishermen busied themselves providing food and drink aplenty for families on both its banks. The climate was kind; never was it bitterly cold for too long in the winter, nor was it unbearably hot during the summer. Snows came and left quickly each year while summer embraced the people with comfortable temperatures for months on end. Along the Miranda there was always a breeze, always some shade, and always a beautiful day not too far away. A place like this was impossible to leave behind, so they stayed.

-=∃⊨-

The villagers could only speculate that the Glazier flew down from the mountains. Often they questioned how their own god would share his home with such a villain. Some of their clan wondered if the beast was sent to impose divine punishment. And for what? Others pretended to know that the evil creature lived in the deepest, coldest parts of the river itself. Neither theory had ever been proven. It seemed the only certainty was that it *would* attack again. No one knew when. No one knew why.

As time went by, Elijah only saw the creature fly over his land one more time during his long and glorious life. His generation was a lucky one. Since they were not being harvested, families grew quite large in number. It was during this time of peace, Kelchi's grandfather raised a son he named Tiko.

In those days, it was not uncommon to change a lad's name. A child's behavior was observed for months and sometimes years until a family's head of household at last recognized an appropriate sobriquet. Tiko, meaning, "happy one, friendly one", was the appropriate name into which Kelchi's father would grow.

The children of Tiko's era enjoyed wonderful years, a time of peace and plenty. Like most toddlers, Tiko was curious and did a lot of questioning, exploring and collecting along with a great deal of listening. Elijah often marveled at the numbers of questions Tiko would bring to him as they sat around the family fire, as they worked together in the fields tending crops, and while the two repaired nets together near the water.

Elijah once commented, "Perhaps, my little happy one, I have misnamed you! Perhaps Salar meaning 'Inspector' would have been better suited for you", and Tiko would laugh with his father as the elder tousled his son's hair.

Topics for discussion ranged from wildlife to sharing items and stories with other children; from fishing to stars in the sky at night; from seasons of the year to the most difficult topic of them all: the monster. Elijah knew the day would come when Tiko would ask him about the winged beast, for Tiko had attended the village fires and heard the songs. Elijah thought he would be prepared for the moment, but he wasn't.

Another day had come to an end. The catch from the river was abundant, and dinner was enjoyed by their fire. Keshishian women were legendary as well. Their skills with fire and food made their men even more willing to hunt and fish.

Their meal by the fire of logs and red-orange coals was peppered with conversation. Much of it was about preparation for winter. Belly nearly full, young Tiko spoke softly, as if the subject he was about to broach deserved a gentle tone.

"Father, do you have time to talk to me now?" Tiko loved dinnertime for it was a time all three of them sat together for more than a few minutes. His mother, Ethella, was renown throughout the village as being dedicated to her two males, and she was an excellent cook. As a young Keshishian, Ethella had listened well among the gatherings of the womenfolk, and learned the many secrets of the local seasonings and herbs. When Elijah took Ethella as his life partner, he knew he would be enjoying meals for many years to come. The muscular appearances of father and son were evidence of her prowess.

Admired for his wisdom even as a younger adult, Elijah was difficult to catch off guard, but he wasn't ready for what his son was about to query. Gazing at his pride and joy, Elijah smiled and uttered softly in return, "I try always to have time for you and your mother. What's on your mind, little one?" Elijah passed some bread to Ethella, and they exchanged the look of a lifetime of love.

As only the young of any culture can be, Tiko was innocently direct. "Near the edge of the forest my friends and I overheard some older boys talking about sentries and a monster as if it might be real." Tiko still chewed the remainder of his fish slowly, but he did not let it keep him from continuing. "I've heard the Teller's ballads, of course, but never thought about them being entirely true."

Elijah waited and thought. "What question do you have?"

"What are sentries and what were they talking about when they mentioned a monster? It seemed they were arguing about it...about whether or not it was imaginary." At this point, the boy's eyes were wide with curiosity, and his boyish wonder reminded his father of the night he himself had questioned Jacar about this very topic a generation earlier.

Ethella made motherly and feeble attempts to alter the topic of their conversation. She commented on the forest and how beautiful it looked each year at this time. She even asked her son if he had noticed the traditional signs of autumn. Ethella asked Tiko if he knew of any woods lore.

"What do you know of the leaves and their colors, my son? Do the other boys know why such events take place?" She listened for a reply from her son, but he was too intent on Elijah and awaited his father's reply.

Elijah smiled knowingly at Ethella. Her attempt at diversion was appreciated and did, indeed, afford him the time to quickly consider what to say to his inquisitive son. To his wife he spoke respectfully.

"It's time, Mother. Thank you." Putting down his food, he gestured for Tiko to sit by his side even closer to the fire. He loved his son, and he wanted this moment to be special.

"Are you comfortable?" he asked in an attempt to gather more precious seconds with which he could continue to gather his thoughts.

"Yes, Father."

By dinner's end, day had grown into twilight. Outside, songs of the elders floated in the air. Stringed instruments and a softly-beaten, hollow log accompanied the singing. This was the time of night and time of year when villagers gathered for song. They knew all too well that soon they would be feeling winter's breath; such traditional gatherings would be scarce during the days and long nights to come. This was the season of singing. Ethella walked outside through the arched doorway to join the clan, closing the cover behind her.

Inside their thatched house, the portals were barely open due to the cool breezes off the river this time of year. Warmed by their fire, Elijah summoned the special words he sought. Young Tiko believed his parent's words were important, and he also knew that what he was about to hear might only be spoken once. His father held his attention.

"Tiko, my father had this talk with me years ago when I was a bit younger than you are tonight. I, too, had overheard other boys discussing a horrible monster, a beast that might attack our people. Like yourself, my ears perked up, my curiosity demanded truth, and I wanted to know more."Elijah paused long, wondering in which direction he would steer his explanation. Something in the traditional village songs being sung in the distance assured him the time was right for this father-son talk. The songs were of his people, and they were the byproduct of tradition. What Elijah was about to share with Tiko was no less customary and certainly no less important. Perhaps his father Jacar before him spoke these same words as he explained the Glazier as well. All Keshishian fathers believed such conversations between father and son should be shared generation after generation.

"Tiko, we are a people of tradition," he continued. "A proud heritage binds us." Having said that, a feeling of pride ran through Elijah, and finally he knew exactly what to say to his son.

"Son, there *is* a monster which threatens our people. As in our stories and songs, our elders have long referred to it as the Glazier." Elijah paused and gently cuddled his son. "As a man I must deal with its existence. As a lad you must deal with it in your own way."

"How, Father?" Tiko wanted to inquire, but Elijah's visage signaled that he should not interrupt.

"It is your duty to your clan to listen when we speak of the monster...the Glazier. What we tell you can and will save the lives of your family and perhaps the lives of others as well."

Elijah gazed across the room lighted by the fire upon some fixed point. It helped him to focus and remember his own father's words, and he was able to continue.

"The Glazier shows no preference when it comes to choosing its victims. It attacks both the young and the old. For this reason, all our people of Keshishia must constantly be prepared. After years of peace, it is easy to forget how important it is to be on guard, but you can help." Elijah stopped speaking and stared into his son's eyes. Tiko understood he was now permitted to speak if he wished.

At that moment, Elijah's candor made Tiko feel older and more mature. Tiko suddenly wanted to begin acting and speaking like a young man of whom the entire village could be proud. The boy began to choose his words carefully and finally realized he was doing so because his father, a well-respected clansman himself, had just this moment told Tiko that he could be of some help. In his boyish enthusiasm, Tiko began to stand up, but Elijah gently pulled him closer to his side.

"Father, what am I to do to help us most?"

Elijah was more proud of his son at this moment than at any other he could remember. Elijah hoped he, too, had made his own father equally as proud, for the entire clan believed that at moments such as this the spirits of elders such as Jacar were present.

"My son, someday we'll travel together through the forest. By then I hope I'll have a plan, and you will be an important part of it."

Tiko somehow knew that the conversation about the Glazier was over for the night. He also sensed his father's plan would be of substance and not whimsical. At last, together they stood and walked into the night, joining the villagers in song.

Years passed and Tiko grew to be a young man. His father's reputation continually grew as well. Elijah's views were respected at Council whenever weighty issues concerning the village were discussed. At one such meeting, several of the elders were again discussing the constant threat from the Glazier. Generation after generation, no one was ever able to predict when the great winged beast might attack again. For that reason, all agreed that a state of readiness was prudent. However, such a state of preparedness was emotionally and mentally draining upon those most responsible for a high level of alert. Sentries were honorable men, and they were treated accordingly. Despite being on a rotation, the position and subsequent responsibilities grew wearisome. Day after day without sightings for years on end, made some wonder if the Glazier still existed. That kind of thinking, the Council warned, was dangerous to all.

"Are we doing all we can to support the sentries?" asked Elijah. His question came from the darker recesses of Council Hall. Seats near the central fire were saved for the elders, and it was near the fire where most discussion took place. To hear a voice from the back of the hall wasn't a difficult task, just an unusual one.

The Council and observers turned toward Elijah who was not at all uncomfortable with their attention and stares. Crackling from the fire was all that was heard and bright sparks flew. Henor, who was generally accepted as the village's eldest statesman, finally spoke.

"How could we help our sentries more than we do? We provide them with fresh replacements and foods. Are not our weapon supplies checked often and kept up to date?"

Again there was quiet. It was a respectful solitude. None at Council felt uncomfortable with the time that passed before anyone spoke again. It was customary to think before speaking. Elijah epitomized the custom. At long last, he spoke again.

"Perhaps we haven't tapped all of our village's resources or harnessed all of our strengths."

Henor once again replied. "If you can suggest how we can provide more strength and offer helpful alternatives, please proceed. How is it possible, Elijah?" The personal address was deemed a sign of respect.

Elijah was standing and moving slowly toward the central fire's light. All eyes were upon him as he spoke. The ease in his manner and tone in which he spoke to Council was admired by all in attendance. "Let us become the hunters and bring an end to being the hunted."

To say the least, more than a murmur was the result at this suggestion. Keshishians were an efficient people, not prone to violence, yet not unfamiliar with a hunt, this is true. But for anyone to suggest their game should become the

Glazier was more than a bold suggestion. Eventually voices quieted, and the great fire of the Council could be heard as it snapped again and again. Shadows danced as if holding everyone in a trance.

At long last, Henor stroked his gray beard and spoke. His was a voice deep and smooth. "Elijah, this is not a new idea. As a young man, I once heard it proposed to Council." His voice carried clearly, and the pace at which he spoke was comfortable for all. When he paused, he was given the courtesy of silence. If Henor wished for others to speak, he would call for them to do so. When he didn't, everyone knew he would eventually speak again. Shadows danced, the blaze crackled, and every member of the clan waited patiently. Again, he spoke. "Were you aware such an idea had been proposed in the past, Elijah?"

By this time, Elijah had settled closer to the fire. No one was offended. He, too, had earned the courtesy of silence. "No, Henor, I was not, but I would be honored if you would share all that you recall."

At length, the head of Council spoke to his people of their ancestors. He told them how they, too, had thought about becoming more of an aggressor.

"Our numbers were few compared to the clan we have today, but mostly we feared leaving our families defenseless. Not everyone was capable of such a hunt. To come back to carnage would have been more than our souls could have withstood." Then he added, "And just as much we were daunted by one question: 'Where do we begin?' "

"I think we can protect those we leave behind." Elijah paused only briefly. "Our winter camps are when we are least vulnerable. Is that not true?"

Elijah saw and heard the agreement. He managed to capture the interest of all those around him. It gave him confidence to continue. Far in the back, Tiko knew he was about to hear the plan of which his father spoke years ago. Interlocking his arm in hers, he held his mother close.

"Let us consider a winter hunt. Let us leave our people behind inside, not in the open. Let us provide for them enough food and firewood to keep them safe."

Now Elijah paused for effect. "And let us hunt only so long as it is not a threat for those in camp. We must agree to return before their supplies run out."

There was quiet. As always, there was consideration. But Elijah had more to say. "To do nothing has proven to be far more dangerous than what I propose, and my own son Tiko would be among those who hunt the beast."

Elijah's plan was eventually granted further discussion. After many more Council meetings, it was agreed that most village sentries would remain to do their work. No one did it better. It was agreed, too, that hunters were needed. Men of skill hopefully would not only find and eventually slay the Glazier, but bring back game from the hunt to restock supplies.

⊰≓≓⊱

Fall became early winter and the great day came. Elijah watched his son closely as he prepared that morning for his departure. Before leaving their house, Ethella and Elijah embraced their son. Similar scenes played out in nineteen other lodges.

"You once asked me what you could do to help. Now you know. I have prepared you over the years as best I knew how," then Tiko's father paused. "I sometimes have questioned whether or not I have been asking you to do too much. There is no greater responsibility than protecting your clan and family." That admission from his father made Tiko feel like a man who had earned his father's highest level of respect.

"We can do this, Father," he quietly replied. Then they embraced once more and exited to meet the others, leaving behind the safety of their log-hewn home with a thickly thatched roof.

By the river the villagers of Keshishia sang again, but this was a song of goodbye. As the brave hunters left, stocked for weeks of passage, everyone could see the snow in the mountains was awaiting them. The river valley was brown, not white with the first snow as of yet. High above, sentries rang their bells to honor those sent upon the hunt. It was the only time anyone recalled hearing the bells toll since they had been put in place nearly a century ago.

⧉

Up in the mountains the weather was dangerous; worse than all had imagined. Each night for eight nights, camp was set among the trees for protection. On the ninth day out, faster men serving as advanced scouts brought back good news. Not far ahead, just below the ledges, were caves large enough to house them all. Scouts suggested that within the caves fires could make the night more bearable.

However, there was more to report: the caves were strewn with bones, the bones of men and larger animals. Fearless and a little desperate for good shelter, twenty Keshishian hunters trudged forward in knee-deep snow, moving upward to a shelter where they could benefit from a night's rest.

Once their fires were started, Tiko and his friends began to shed some of their garb. Fire starters experienced the worst. It was they who had to gather the wood, shards for kindling and logs for fire, but worst of all was removing their shoulder length gloves so that they could work with their hands more efficiently. The cold was bitter, and they worked quickly. Their reward was that none of them had to stand guard through the night. It was agreed they were permitted to sleep in the deepest, warmest recesses the cave.

As the darkness was warded off by the blaze of their camp-fires, fifty feet away winter winds howled across the entrance. The opening was not much larger than two men; however, it led to a sizeable cavern deep within the mountain. They had agreed to stay together as one group in the largest cave, for being divided appealed to no one.

Provisions were shared, and stories were told. Stories were a Keshishian tradition. Eventually, however, the topic on everyone's mind finally came to the surface. Were their weapons sufficient, and where exactly were they going to continue their hunt? And why were there so many bones inside the cave?

Henor's son Laria was one of the hunters. He sat near all the men, not far from the fire, and next to him was Tiko. Quietly Laria discussed how their weapons had long been enough to provide for their people. He felt confidence in their skill to use them.

"All of us have used the nets, our bows and spears, as well as our slings. Before we left our families, we checked each other's gear. We know we're amply supplied."

Tiko joined in with his friend. "We all have our doubts, but they must be quelled with confidence. Is there one among us who has not felt the fear of letting down his people when out on a hunt for food?" He looked about the blaze, and all nodded in agreement.

"We must face this new fear in the same manner." Then there was the customary quiet. Tiko had known each of these men for his entire life. They were his trusted friends. When he continued he said, "It would be easy to divide our group for searching purposes and plan to meet here nightly, but I suggest to you it would be foolish to do so. We know not our foe. Our strength must lie in numbers."

From the direction of the cave's entrance came the deep voice of Velon, Laria's closest neighbor back in Keshishian. "Doesn't anyone want to discuss the bones?" Velon was replaced as guard by one of the hunters so that he could speak his piece.

"It's obvious that they've long been left here in this place. There is no meat, no flesh, or smell of decadence. But why are they here?" He sat by the fire, glad to have the chance to be warmed. Over the years, his face had become ruddy in complexion from many days of outdoor work in the sun and snow. "They're the bones of not just animals, but those of men as well."

Another added, "Yet there is not one bit of clothing or a single tool to hint who these people might have been." Everyone still awake offered various ideas to explain the presence the skeletal remains.

It was Laria who proposed an idea that chilled them despite the fire's flames. "Perhaps this is the lair of the Glazier. Perhaps it is one of many." Silence was never more pronounced. Was that possible? Had they clumsily stumbled upon the home of the beast, at least one of his hideaways?

"For that to be the case would there not have to be a larger entrance?" At that thought from Velon, much relief was felt for they wanted to believe he was right. The Glazier had always been described as a gigantic, winged beast. Despite this reassurance, most of the men slept fitfully that night.

By dawn the wind had subsided. The sky was overcast, and snow was falling heavily. A few men added bones to their fire, and were about to plan their day. Tiko walked to the cave entrance and called for Malin whose turn it was last to guard the opening. There was no answer. Tiko returned to the fire quickly.

"Where is our brother Malin?" The others understood the tone of his voice. He was obviously concerned. "He's not a fire starter, so he's not out collecting wood." Calls bounced from cavern wall to cavern wall. Malin was nowhere to be found.

Laria and Tiko chose to step outside the cave's entrance to look for prints upon the ledge. Then they peered below in case the young hunter had fallen. Malin was not to be found. Fresh, deep white snow was everywhere, and it was undisturbed.

Looking at Tiko, Laria said, "It's as if he flew off from here." After his words traveled across the crisp, clean air to his friend, both realized immediately what the other was thinking.

Back in the cave by the fire, everyone searched the cavern one final time. Their many voices echoed loudly. No sign of their friend was reported.

Velon spoke. "We must expect the worst." Others were anxious to start a search outside immediately.

Tiko made them wait. "We must organize quickly, but we must be careful all the same." The men agreed again to stay together, but they opted to spread apart at equal distances in order that each hunter could be seen by another to his left or to his right.

Of course, the extreme flanks would have only one partner to account for them. For those positions, Laria and Tiko volunteered. Each man donned his clothing to fight the cold, and made sure his whistle of bone was working correctly. In this snow, a whistle might be the difference between danger and safety. Generations of fathers had taught them that.

All were anxious to reach the summit. They felt that although it might be dangerous and would challenge their energy, the peak would give them the best possible view of the area.

Along the way they found more caves and more bones. In one cave, in particular, one with a larger opening, were Malin's remains. His corpse was still unfrozen. He had died not long before he was discovered. Whistles were sounded to call in all the hunters, and fire starters began what they did best.

Combined with the wood that fueled the fire, Malin's remains released a darkened plume against the bright, gray sky of noonday. His ashes were ceremoniously spread across the snow from a ledge not far from the cave entrance. There was little conversation. Enthusiasm for the hunt had been nearly abashed. At last, some re-suggested the caves might indeed be a lair for the beast and shared their concern that if they camped inside any of them, they might be little more than bait. From that discussion, they formulated a plan.

—◦❧❧◦—

The Glazier was larger than stories recalled. Over the years, it seemed to prefer the cover of darkness, so ancestors really were hard pressed to gauge its size. That very night before it flew toward the peaks surrounding Keshishian, ready to attack once again the unsuspecting village below, it caught the scent of something unfamiliar; unfamiliar but appealing. The beast was hungry.

Wings arched, riding thermals up the side of the mountain, it turned its triangular-shaped head toward the scent. The Glazier veered north and flew silently; its raptor talons itched for flesh. Easily the leathery-winged monster was of far greater size than the condors often seen flying above the Miranda each spring. Condors were easily 20 feet in length from wing tip to wing tip and amazingly fast when diving for prey. The Glazier was not only faster and larger, but evidently built for battle with nature's elements since its skin was so thick yet supple. An occasional beating of its wings thrust it toward a billow of smoke not more than a mile away.

The hunters worked quickly and carefully. They knew not if cremating one of their own would draw the beast in their direction, but it was agreed that Malin would have been proud to have been part of the plan.

Nineteen hunters worked together as one in order to effectively prepare for the raptor's attack. They did not know when it would return or if it would return, but agreed it was foolish to think otherwise especially if they planned on camping in its lair through yet another long, wintry night.

While on watch, Velon was the first to spot the tremendous creature. At first he was uncertain, for the cloud coverage at the summit, combined with the snowfall made spotting objects difficult. At the shrill of his whistle, the others took their places. Readying for battle, never before had the weapons of these hunters been grasped so tightly.

The raptor was quick to detect motion not far from the source of the dark smoke. Momentarily it was torn between its natural instinct to attack the living prey below or to investigate the source of the enticing scent that appealed to it, from miles way. Hunger took over.

The scream from the wild bird was equal to its legendary reputation. As Velon retreated to the cave's entrance, the screeching blast from the giant's mouth caused snow to fall from the mountain's ledge, making it more difficult for Velon to run to the safety of the cave. Seeing this, Laria and the rest shot arrows toward the attacker. A quick dive saved Velon from certain death. Since the icy, stone ledge protruded far enough from the mountainside, it forced the Glazier to alter its path.

So intense was the pain inflicted by their weapons as it flashed through the torso of the great beast, it screeched even more loudly a scream heretofore unknown to the human ear; loud enough to cause its adversaries below to wince.

Rage painted its mind, and considering its size the Glazier reversed its path so much more adeptly than anyone thought possible. In an instant, the raptor scraped up a victim from the mountainside and dashed his life instantly with a powerful tightening of its talons. The creature's beak wildly did the rest. So quickly did all of this happen that a scream was never heard from its victim. Eighteen remained.

Angry yelling and screaming distracted the savage monster from its temporary thirst for blood. Reminded there were more humans to devour, from a nearby, cragged ledge upon which it had perched the Glazier released their comrade's body to the ground far below. As the tiniest oriole might hop from branch to branch, this monster moved from one snow-covered rock ledge to another, positioning for attack.

Then came down the nets! Having covered themselves with several feet of snow, Laria and Tiko had waited until the beast was just below them on the shelf outside the cave. Weighted with large rocks, one net made from twenty, tightened around the giant's flapping, leather wings as it angrily tried to extricate itself. Five men below the frantic creature reined in the ropes extending from the bottom of the snare as eleven remaining marksmen emptied their quivers into the belly of the beast. Ice, snow, and rocks flew all about them as the hardened talons and tremendous beak attempted to make escape a possibility. Its screeching was horrific. The more they gathered in the netting to trap it against the face of the small cave entrance, the easier their enemy was to spear. The dying raptor was too large for the opening where it had tossed its other victims from days gone by.

Silence. Footsteps were few, for no one dared risk being wrong about the death of this foe. To let go prematurely seemed to risk letting the bird come back to life. The enraged hunters of Keshishia continued to stab at their game, each twisting his own spear point harshly as if to be certain its fight to live was over. As one they screamed until they were too exhausted to scream anymore.

The sheer weight of the creature tore at the tie downs securing the netting from above. As a result, Laria and Tiko were nearly yanked down the mountainside as well! Tiko grabbed for his partner as he was about to plummet to his death. With Laria's collar in hand, Tiko whistled on the bone whistle his father had carved for him as a young hunter years ago. Conditions were treacherous, but help arrived in time, providing necessary assistance as Laria dangled above the dead Glazier's carcass two hundred feet below. The battle was over.

***

The new tale was told. In the peaceful days that followed, after chores were done, Kelchi and his young friends roamed the banks of the Miranda as an imaginary army, brave and true. By decree, a new Keshishian ballad had become its best and was to be sung, forever exalting the men they knew personally, men who made a more peaceful lifestyle possible for all. Now honor was to be earned not by fighting, but by preserving the safe Keshishian lifestyle which had become theirs to pass on to their descendants.

*** The following story is dedicated to the many readers who have requested a sequel to my first novel <u>Birds on aWire</u>. Enjoy!

HERE WE GO AGAIN

'Twas but a few years ago he came within a whisker of losing them all, and they nearly lost him as well.

ON FRIDAY MORNING, RITA'S HUSBAND left earlier than usual. As she worked at her computer in what Eli called her office, she looked out their window to greet what looked to be another beautiful morning. From her comfortable leather seat, she could see the gravel road he had taken to work. The bumpy road surface was an acceptable tradeoff for the increased privacy they desired which they found on a remote piece of property not too far outside of her home town of Falls Port.

In the moonlight, Jette Lake Trail was a charcoal gray path as it curled through nearby trees and fields until it disappeared in the distance. By day? By day it was nothing more than gravel, but it was *their* gravel. She smiled a miniscule smile when she recalled his daily ritual of honking his red truck's horn three times, that old, red Dodge Dakota they hung on to for so many years. Three honks...three words: "I love you." Friday morning had been no different.

His new work paid well, but troubleshooting technology required that he travel in a pretty wide circle. Rita Parks crossed her fingers when she learned that a sizeable portion of his commute was to be spent driving his truck to job sites.

For romantic reasons, he would not part with it, nor would Rita ask him to do so. A guy was supposed to have fond memories of his favorite vehicles. Each was a rung upon a ladder, and this one had supported him well at key moments in his life. In Eli's mind, the Dakota was part of them, and soon he planned to pass it along to his son Jake.

After a sip of coffee, Rita hopped up from her desk to check on him as he slept. Jake was self-sufficient, of course, but he had been through so much that she couldn't help watching over him more than some step moms might have done. Protective? Perhaps. Four years passed since his mother's murder, but Rita intended to stay nearby whenever she could. Jake was asleep. Rita smiled and pursed her lips as her next thoughts drifted to Ed.

She, too, had brought a son to her marriage with Eli, but Edward had moved out on his own, albeit not too far away. He was in Somers upon the big lake's western shore. Soon Jake would spread his wings too, so she was determined to enjoy his company until that day arrived.

The three men in her life were wonderful together. Mutual respect and good-natured teasing quickly bonded them as one. Their most recent team project had been the resurrection of an old, wall-mounted intercom. Rita had not come to trust it completely even though it was Eli who repaired it under the supervision of his sons. A lot of teasing was exchanged over that family project. He often repaired expensive modern technology, but occasionally older gadgets gave Eli fits. Sometimes the intercom worked, and sometimes it did not.

Besides family? Rita knew Eli's passion was his work. It mattered not to him whether it was on a local hospital's equipment, a bank system across Lake County, or his own truck. He simply enjoyed his occupation.

Back at her desk, she recalled an unusual autumn night when he had to jury rig his truck with some airplane parts which he snagged from a local pilot days earlier. Eli just thought parts of anything were interesting, no matter the technology's era. As his pile of collectibles grew, he was heard to say many times, "I'll never know when I might need one of these!" On this particular snowy night, everyone was happy he saved them.

"Oh what a night," she pondered. While returning from Kalispell's airport, he hit ice on 93 S, skidding dangerously close to the edge of the steep highway before coming to rest head-on against a protective stone wall. His headlights had been smashed. Losing his lights was bad, but the wall might well have prevented an uglier scenario had he flown over the bank below.

Rita walked back into their bedroom and sipped more coffee as she continued her recalling that night in October not so long ago. The weather was bad, even for a Montana fall. No one else was out and about, and Eli wanted desperately to be home. It was Edward's birthday, and he wanted to join in the celebrating.

Ordinarily Cessna lights would be too bright under normal conditions, but since no one else was on the road, and since he was still twenty-five miles from their home, Eli accepted the risk. He pitied any unfortunate drivers who might come in his direction, because there are no low beams on the lights of an airplane.

Home at last, exhausted from being so careful, more friends were there than he expected. Four wheelers and snowmobiles decorated the yard. Edward had enjoyed his favorite foods with his buddies, and all were relieved when Eli returned. Edward, Jake and all of their friends sat around to hear his story as Rita served him a meal she kept warm.

He spoke of how the Cessna lights illuminated the wind-driven pieces of snow. "They weren't flakes, and they weren't ice. It's hard to describe." He added to his tale by saying, "They were nearly mesmerizing - almost hypnotic."

Now, many months later, while relaxing in the window seat of their bedroom, she remembered more of his words from that night, and how he recalled the snow on the mountain was unlike any snow that fell in the valleys. "It was sugar-like in consistency; a dry snow and not flakey at all." He spoke of how he could actually hear the snow "pouring like sugar" all around him as he scrambled to fasten the powerful lights to this truck while holding a flashlight in his mouth.

Jake's words came to mind. "Thank God you're an engineer, Dad. I doubt many people would have thought to attempt what you did." Then he laughed. "And thank God you didn't fry the electrical system on *my* truck!"

Rita finished her lukewarm drink as she imagined again how it must have been peacefully quiet on top of the mountain. She admired her husband because he had recalled the event not as terrible or inconvenient but rather an experience that was brimming with beauty. They both loved nature, as did both of their sons. A proper respect for the great outdoors helped make Montana the best place for them to call "home".

His *bride* as he still called her, delighted in remembering little gestures, like when her hubby hustled home to surprise her with an early return from work. Many a day they walked along their lake as a couple, leading to a favorite spot along the shore. They sat side-by-side on the ground holding hands, and or upon a log where he would massage Rita's neck.

One of his successful home projects involved restoring an aluminum folding chair in order that she might sit by the lake and write. Many were the days she hiked to that very spot by herself and took comfort in it. When finished relaxing, she simply left the little green and white seat along the shoreline. The weather couldn't hurt it, and there were no visitors who would run off with it. Oh! Rita heard Jake moving about, so from her reveries she did return.

The Dakota was running fine, and Eli never seemed to mind his commutes. "It's much better I travel all around Lake County than continue to circumnavigate the rest of the planet," he was fond of saying. Formerly an engineer working inside the U.S. Naval Warfare Center in D.C., those travels were extensive and cost his first marriage and nearly cost him his life. Now a resident of rural Montana, he was learning how to relax.

Eli understood that not everyone enjoyed his or her livelihood as much as he enjoyed his own. One of his teachers once told him that people should find something they like to do, and then they should figure out a way to get paid for doing it. Spanning both his careers, the one in D.C. and the next in Montana, he was able to do just exactly that: enjoy his work.

"Most people don't want to get their hands dirty, Rita. Or they are afraid they won't be able to fix what is wrong. I love to work with my head and my hands, repair things, and I have found there's good money in doing it." Deep inside, Rita enjoyed having her repairman handy as well.

She sat down and continued her work at her computer. When Jake needed lunch, there would be little time for journalism. Montana's northwest newspaper, *The Daily Inter Lake* for whom she worked, did not mind if she worked at home. However, a deadline was a deadline.

⊰⧕⧔⊱

Friday wasn't too bad. Kalispell and Missoula airports were his most common stopping points, but occasionally he was lucky enough to schedule some work at Falls Port's local landing strip not far from home. Working there on the smaller planes or office technology afforded him the opportunity to return home ahead of time.

He surely loved his family, and returning home had taken on a new level of importance. 'Twas but a few years ago he came within a whisker of losing them all, and they nearly lost him as well. Back then he was still in D.C. Fortunately, good friends like President Rittenhouse, and local resident Alan Wing who grew up with Rita were able to come to their aid. Whenever those events crept back into his mind, Eli shuddered to think what transpired. Unwittingly he had put them through such an emotional grind.

Back in the day, his engineering missions demanded that he alleviate any qualms he possessed regarding all sorts of travel, for over a million miles had been travailed via jets, fast cars, and submarines. Secretive, spur-of-the-moment journeys requiring long flights were not uncommon, so he thought it ironic that a crash near Falls Port in a Cessna abated his desire to fly. Lucky for others he had not abandoned his love of machinery, including planes. He understood the technology and folks relied on his talents, but he need not go up in the air.

Bob DiGiallonardo was the airport's owner/ manager as well as the airport café's short-order cook. He often teased Eli, "Paisano, if I could afford to hire you full time, I would." Then he'd laugh and ask, "Would you consider working for meals?" Together the two would joke and dream about the day it might happen.

For a while, pulling into the airport overlooking Falls Port was almost too much. Flashbacks deluged his consciousness. Flashing lights, sirens, and a myriad of harried voices were still vivid memories. The thoughts of the crash and subsequent images were all too similar to the *first* spot of trouble involving his friend the President. However, Eli eventually learned to cope and was back once again harassing his new friend Bob.

Friday's weather was glorious and he hoped to be home by mid- afternoon to enjoy one of their spontaneous hikes by the lake. On this day, however, it wasn't to be. One of the airport's regulars needed to leave for Boise, Idaho in the morning to see his alma mater's Boise State Broncos play the BYU Cougars upon the beautiful blue football field for which the team first became famous. It was up to Eli to make the flight happen. He called Rita, and as always she understood.

"Your dad's gonna be late tonight, Jake. It's you and me unless Ed shows up. When you're the best at what you do, the world demands your help." After a pause, she added, "They want you 24/7."

From another room, Jake could be heard laughing mildly at his step mother's attempt to be cool. He thought it odd to hear her use what was already an old-fashioned catchphrase. "Before you know it," he chided from down the hall, "you'll be clicking that intercom and saying '10-4'!"

"If it works!" she replied in a humorous volley.

"Touché", he laughed.

Eli, too, teased her about it when she tried to use such phrases. "That newspaper is ruining your vocabulary," he poked, knowing full well that the paper had nothing to do with it. Rita knew her husband was supportive and that he was proud of her writing as well. She missed teaching some days, but having turned that page of her life's story, she was thoroughly enjoying the newspaper as a journalist and illustrator.

Day had passed, and the light that gently flowed out of their living room's bay window cast nearly a golden hue. From the outside, the turn-of-the-century farmhouse exuded country charm. Having left on some lights at the top of the stairs, their home was a scene for Currier and Ives or a candidate for a Norman Rockwell print.

The flat-screen television was on, and it sat among books and small figurines upon their white, built-in shelves, by the window. The local news anchor reported that an escapee from the State Court House might possibly be at large in their surrounding Lake County area. Locals were advised to use extreme caution, as the man was considered dangerously violent.

"Mom, are you hearing this?" Jake called to Rita.

"Helena is three to four hours from here, Jake." She knew Jake was still grasping local geography since he moved in with them not so long ago from Pennsylvania. "I hope he can't run *that* far away." She stood in the archway listening to the report while suppressing some old worrisome thoughts of her own.

As it ended, she turned to the kitchen, walking right by the alarm system to the left of their four-paneled front door. For a microsecond, she considered setting the alarm, but anticipating Eli's return she neglected to bother. Her mind was focused on what they would have for dinner.

Having left her glasses by her computer, she quickly trotted up the risers to her office. From there Rita was able to hear the most recent update regarding the escaped killer. She listened closely as the reporter described the daring escape that had been executed earlier that day.

"On the way to the trial, Vincent 'Vinnie' Formica, accused of alleged violent crimes against his victims, including attempted murder, had feigned a serious injury by cutting himself with a knife. He purposefully cut himself just below his eye which produced a lot of blood although it wasn't a serious wound.

"It seems it was cleverly done more for effect," the anchor elaborated, "and it worked, for a sympathetic guard momentarily forgot the demeanor of his captive. When he attempted to assist, the officer became victim of the very same knife!" Upon the couch, Jake was glued to the reportage, for he had witnessed firsthand such ugliness before.

"Where," Rita called to her step son, "would a dangerous inmate gain access to a knife?" She walked by the intercom expecting a reply. Perhaps Jake felt hers was a rhetorical question, for he never said a word in return. "God help us," she whispered.

While at the top of the steps, she peeked at her computer screen to see whether or not she had received any new assignments from her editor. Finding nothing, she flicked off the bathroom light at the stop of the stairs, and returned down the stairway to their cozy kitchen just off the living room.

He was a huge man. Colossal! He held Jake in his grasp. His mouth covered by the escapee's fat hand, Jake's chest was heaving. In a flash, she realized how the horrible man standing in front of her probably experienced no struggle at all when he knifed and murdered that poor guard earlier in the day. Now the monster was in their home and held poor Jake captive.

Fear nearly caused her to faint. Her knees actually buckled. Suddenly he tossed Jake to the floor and lunged for Rita, wrapping his massive forearm around her throat. His strength was not a surprise. She thought of how easy it would be for him to twist her neck at any moment if he so desired. She feared what he desired was worse.

From the kitchen floor, Jake looked up but said nothing. Eyes large, he watched as their captor kept a strong grasp on the new mother he had grown to love. Rita found his dirty, calloused hand offensive, for it reeked of dried, red fluid. The animal hadn't even take time to wash off the blood of the guard rendered lifeless earlier that day.

In a voice that was as gravelly as the road to their house, he pointed at Jake and commanded him a menacing tone. "Get yourself into that closet!"

Jake was torn. Of course, he wanted to help Rita with a sudden courageous attack, but thinking better of the idea, he decided it might be safer for both of them to do as he was told.

Once in the closet, he heard it being barricaded by furniture, followed by the smashing of lamps and shades which no longer stood upon tables at either end of their couch. To accomplish such vandalism, Jake hoped the monster was forced to release Rita, and she was free to run.

But Rita, too, moved little. She stifled her crying in the hopes it might help their cause. She had talked and reasoned with difficult kids when she taught in her school but, of course, those situations were nothing like this.

Stumbling about as if he knew not what to do next, he found her again in a corner. The creature wrapped the crude texture of his large arm around her shoulders and paused as if considering his very next move. Rita cringed when she felt his rough hand move up to her throat, but then he proceeded to throw her to the floor. Temporarily he searched for a light switch, eventually found it, and plunged the room into darkness.

Mind and body were at work. Her heart beat explosively against the walls of her chest as it constricted and made each breath a difficult task. Her own little hands became clammy with sweat, powerless against such a beast. Thoughts of her husband raced through her head, and for an instant her brain summoned Alan, a classmate who saved her life years ago.

"How can this be happening?" she thought to herself. "Were we *meant* to die tonight?" She began to sob but stifled it with a series of short staccato breaths that were sufficient to keep her alert.

Dragged to the back of the darkened kitchen, Rita recognized its familiar shadows created by the moonlight. It was then that she saw the knife, naught but a toy in his mammoth hand it seemed. Weakening from fear, the size of the ogre amazed her once again. Like pin balls under glass, her eyes darted rapidly seeking any trace of light. Blues and reds from a television show added a surrealistic touch. She thought of her family, especially Jake stuffed into the coat closet, wondering if he had already been stabbed.

Sapped of her strength, Rita struggled to stand and somehow was able to do so. "Don't do this! Please do *not* do this!" she begged as he came at her forcefully still wielding that knife.

The blade was put to her throat, glistening in the moonlight. He grabbed Rita by her waist and violently spun her body around, placing her back against his chest. Pulling her in closer, he whispered into her ear, but all she heard were the three honks of their truck!

The invader grunted like a bear and once again pushed Rita Parks down to the floor. Eyes closed, she saw jagged white flashes when the back of her head slammed against a hard cabinet door. Irritated by the interruption, he looked down the road toward the sound of Eli's pickup. His continuous grunting was visceral. His massive silhouette filling the door, to Rita he appeared even more menacing standing there not far away. She imagined he was deciding who to kill first. Adrenaline brought her back to her knees.

Once he ripped their phone off the wall she knew he had made up his mind. No calls could be made if he slipped outside to hunt down her husband, and the element of surprise would make Eli an easy prey. But he just couldn't abandon her, for surely she'd begin to cry out. The huge beast of a man realized his options, and despite the darkness she saw what was coming. A huge fist sent her to the floor one final time and into a deeper darkness.

Seconds earlier, Eli's eyes left the road as he glanced at their home in the distance. Proud of it, he loved driving up Jette Lake Trail at night, looking across the small body of water, and seeing the lights pouring out of their windows.

"Odd," he thought. "The lights aren't on," but he noted the glow of their T V. It was then as he did every night, he honked his horn three times.

The Dodge lumbered up the driveway and passed the front walk which led to their old wooden steps. What was once a small barn had become the garage he desired for his truck and the many items he collected during his travels. It wasn't pretty, but he and their sons did a good enough job to suit Eli.

As he removed his keys from the ignition, he grabbed his paperwork and his thermos. Carefully he stepped down from the cab. Above the noise of the truck door being shut, he heard a static-filled, crackling sound. He was certain it was electrical in nature. For a split second, he thought he heard Jake's voice and then Rita's as well.

"Is that the intercom?" he whispered to himself in mild surprise. His first inclination was to think they were teasing him, considering the number of times he'd tried to repair the gadget in the past. "The thing's actually working!" It was crackling, but he finally figured out what they were frantically saying. Were they joking or were they serious?

"Eli! There's a man...a huge, horrible man someplace outside the house!"

More static followed, but then he clearly heard, "...wants to kill us, Dad! Be careful!" The fear in their voices convinced him he had better regard their warnings as serious. "Please, Dad. Don't let him kill us."

Seconds later the intercom cut out. The subsequent hush was nearly as harrowing as their warning, but the silence made the giant's now-audible footsteps easy to recognize, for gravel underfoot has its own unique sound.

Darkness that swallowed the truck enabled Eli to covertly search for a shovel, a rake…anything that would help him protect himself. To pull the light cord dangling above the driver's side door would turn on the light, but reveal his location and make him an easier target. Whoever was outside the garage was on unfamiliar ground, especially if he stepped inside the garage. Sweating profusely, the convict was waiting for his next victim to step out.

With the stealth of Montana mountain lion, Eli finally discovered the axe he used to split kindling. Crouched in defensive stance, he worried that waiting too long or acting too slowly might permit his adversary to return to the house. As dangerous as it was, the thought of the killer's retreat was the impetus Eli needed to step into the moonlight and bravely confront his foe.

Rolling across the lake was an intense, thunderous explosion that echoed off uncounted hillsides far away, the sort of rumble that succeeds jagged white lightning during the worst of storms. The giant of a man, who moments ago held their lives in his hands, never knew what it was that hit him. He never would.

Neither the psychopath nor Eli had any idea that Jake had freed himself from the closet and quickly revived the woman who had become his mom. Employing some skills passed on by his step brother, Jake was able to grab a rifle, load it quickly, and take the necessary steps.

Never before had young Jake Parks killed an elk or a deer let alone another human being. He was more comfortable with a rod and a reel. However, since his move to Montana, target shooting had become a family tradition, enjoyed together on Sundays in the back fields of their home as Rita looked on from her chair. On this Friday night, the target wasn't paper or tin. It was the giant who fell at Dad's feet.

Pop Up

He was made of sterner stuff…demanding.
Quitting was not in his vocabulary.

DURING OUR LIVES, WE MEET all sorts of people. Some have a profound influence upon us while others are hardly noticed as they pass us by like a breeze. To this very day, I enjoy meeting people for the first time. More often than not such encounters have been pleasant experiences.

Curious by nature I ask, "Where is home for you?" If they have traveled far to become a new part of my life, I extend my hand and happily add, "I've never shaken hands with a person from _____ before!" After the exchange of a pleasant handshake, I have often been permitted to pick the brain of the person I just met. By doing so, I hope I've made a new friend and perhaps gained valuable fodder for any upcoming stories I might share.

Sitting behind a table for a book signing or just while sitting upon a park bench in our remote Pennsylvania town, I have shaken hands with folks from faraway states such as Oregon, California, Florida, and Maine to name a few. Other countries? On that list, you will find France, Great Britain, Canada, Ukraine, Japan and others. Inside my head is a map decorated with the tiniest red push pins indicating the homes of all of these many nice people.

Twenty years ago, a former student evidently paid attention as I told my class I enjoyed greeting folks from anywhere. It was one of the many reasons I enjoyed teaching. I spoke of my habit of asking techies, "Where are you sitting right now?" as they helped me repair my computer via a call.

"I don't travel much," I explained to my students, "but my voice has been in countries all around the world."

A year later, I answered the phone in our home not knowing what I was about to hear were words I would *never* forget. From afar, when young Ethan Wallis heard my voice, he immediately said to me, "G'day, Mr. W! I just wanted you to know your voice has now been in Australia!" Wow!

Like most of us, I have met a great number of individuals who have decorated my life with wonderful anecdotes. However, the following tale is about a man who did more than decorate my life. He painted it. Let me tell you about Pop.

I am not sure we ever shook hands; not once in all the years we were together. Maybe we did. I don't remember. However, he certainly had a profound influence upon me as well as many others.

As a point of interest, although it's not at all important to this story, as days and years race by it seems I can see him in my bathroom mirror more easily. According to his sister, my Aunt Olive, he might have been an inch or two taller than I've grown to be and, "He was one handsome man!"

And, yes, I actually have an "Aunt Olive". I feel she's noteworthy for two reasons: She and Uncle Willard were such kind-hearted folks plus it's been my experience that there aren't too many "Aunt Olives". And yes, I actually had an "Uncle Willard", but enough of that. Let's not go down that rabbit trail.

Now keep in mind that Pop had four sons. Ask each of us to recall him, and you might well receive four varied descriptions of the man. That being said, I'll begin by relaying that he was made of sterner stuff. He wasn't mean, and he certainly was not abusive, but he was tough…demanding. If any skill was an issue, practice…correctly orchestrated practice… was the cure. Quitting was not in his vocabulary.

Family stories taught us he was athletic and a talented baseball player. My favorite photo of Pop captured him standing among his teammates who played on Hopewell, New Jersey's town team circa 1928-1935, the very same Hopewell Township where Charles Lindbergh's baby boy was kidnapped and killed in March of 1932. In fact, Pop went on to marry our mother, a woman who went to her grave uncertain as to whether or not she and a close friend gave directions to the kidnaper the night of the crime, but that's another story. In the aforementioned photo, Pop stood tall, sported big ears, and appeared to ooze confidence.

As I remember him, the word *supportive* best described him (once we were past that "stern" issue). If any of us needed to be someplace on time, he made sure he took us there early. When appropriate, he watched us as a spectator, and many times he was even our coach. The only time he deviated from those roles occurred during my tenth-grade year. He chose to be with our mom who was slowly dying of cancer.

Time and how we pass it is an interesting concept to ponder. Pop passed his days as if each hour always had a purpose. From what I witnessed, the man rarely missed a day of work. That might explain why he earned the promotions he did. He climbed the ladder of business from employee to Secretary Treasurer of a Philadelphia company during the late 1950's.

There was that one brief spell when he was subjected to a bone spur surgery which hampered him all throughout the autumn of 1964. The silver lining was that it coincided with my football season, and he never missed a game home or away. I'd peek up toward the bleachers looking for the only guy with crutches, and there he'd be game after game.

I cannot say he attempted to accomplish everything single-handedly. He evidently understood the advantage of working in a group. For example, there was World War II before I was born. He couldn't have defeated Japan on his own!

Of course, I jest. My point is that he worked well with others including our mom. She was straight out of that 1940's-1950's stereotype created by television shows like *Father Knows Best, Ozzie and Harriet,* and *Leave it to Beaver.* She was raising three rambunctious sons years before I ever showed up on her radar, and Mom was a single-mom at least temporarily as she watched Pop go off to war in the South Pacific. Relatives insisted that she loved Pop tremendously, so she pretty much let him set the rules or establish expectations when it came to our behavior. Mom never spared the famous phrase, "Wait 'til your father gets home."

Pop was king of our castle, but there was no doubt she was his queen. That's important to share right here in this story, for they were partners when discipline was required.

One Saturday morning in autumn they discovered I had been playing with matches along with a neighborhood buddy (whose name I won't mention in case his parents read this).

We had been out in the neighboring woods building campfires using twigs and dried leaves as our kindling. It was agreed that the best way to teach me the danger of fire, the pain fire might cause was to hold my hand above his Zippo lighter's blue, orange, and yellow flame. Then I was sentenced to the front porch for the day to "...learn a lesson!" To my knowledge, neither of them buckled and peeked in on me. I sat there for quite some time. I do know this: I never played with fire after that.

I cannot recall Pop ever spanking me, but my older brothers often referred to "the strap" as being a tactical part of their childhood. Yes, Pop hung a leather barber's strap in his closet, and it was easy for all to see; strategically mounted I imagine. I saw it occasionally, but I never understood the need for it. He owned and used an electric razor. As a matter of fact, to my knowledge he never once referred to the strap's existence. I never understood why they thought it was such a big deal. My brothers' unanimous answer? "Pop's mellowed. You don't have the same father we did."

I actually asked him about that one day. "Pop, did Chuck, Larry, or Dave have a different father?" He just chuckled and rubbed the top of my head.

However, there *was indeed* that one day! Their claim was abashed. I had gone too far. Rule #13 came into play: "Do not *EVER* cross the rail road tracks." The tracks were located a mere two blocks down from our home at the end of Grant Avenue. There were two sets of rails to whisk commuters speedily in and out of the city of Philadelphia, crossing the Delaware River not far from where we resided.

Thanks to the intimidation or peer pressure of Billy McGowan, the oldest second grader in the history of Collins Tract School, I crossed the tracks about 3:30 in the afternoon. Earlier during Mrs. Madara's science lesson about frogs, Billy informed me that there were thousands of tadpoles awaiting us "...on the other side." I knew it was a violation of Rule #13, but I had not one clue what a tadpole was. And then, of course, there were these words that came from the mouth of the world's biggest second grader:"Are ya chicken?"

I knew if I didn't go our entire class would ostracize me. And my brothers? If they learned I balked on a dare of this magnitude? I'd never hear the end of it.

"No! I'm not chicken!" and off we journeyed.

I returned home that afternoon covered to my knees in wet clay. It was caked on my dungarees. (We called jeans "dungarees" back then just like we called a couch a "davenport". Don't ask.) Then things unfolded like this:

Phase 1: "Wait 'til your father gets home," Mom dictated.

Phase 2: "He's gonna get the strap! He's gonna get the strap!" bounced off the knotty pine walls of the upstairs dormitory-like bedroom Pop had built for my brothers. Dave was going up the steps two at a time announcing my fate to Chuck and Larry who were doing their homework. Rule #6 ordered that we do homework after school before we go out to play. Apparently, I broke that rule as well.

Phase 3: Pop's arrival. Not in the house two minutes, he was informed of my transgression. He entered my tiny, downstairs bedroom, and I noticed he was carrying the famous strap in his hand. It was a supple leather, about two inches in width, and approximately two feet in length. The leather was a shiny brown.

I was calmly told, "Assume the position" or lie across the bed. Not long after, seconds after I was in position, I heard the strap whoosh through the air. Immediately I heard it make contact, but I felt no pain! He missed! Then he continued to miss repeatedly, and he sternly asked, "Will you cross the tracks again?" With each thwack upon the bed I assured him that I would not! Never once at any time in my life was I struck with the strap (or any device), but that day the bed took a whipping.

As I said, he worked well with others. Lucky for many kids, he and a few other men spearheaded a community-oriented, kid-friendly bunch. During the early fifties these men introduced not only Williamsport's Little League Baseball to Pennsauken, but The Boy Scouts of America and Troop 132 simultaneously.

My older brothers bought into both of these organizations. I did not. I was interested solely in baseball, retiring from Cub Scouts (and all scouting) at the ripe old age of nine. To his credit, even though it surely disappointed him, the only thing Pop ever said to me about my early retirement from scouting was, "How will you ever learn to properly tie knots?" I've never forgotten that, and each time I attempt to fasten something with a rope, I think of his inquiry. However, there was that *one time* before I jumped off the Cub Scout ship...

Each month it seemed that every Cub Scout on the planet assembled in our Police Station's hall to have a Troop Meeting. Until my first meeting, I never knew there were so many dark blue shirts, yellow bandanas, and arrowhead badges.

December rolled around and despite Christmas being close at hand, there was yet another Troop Meeting. This one, however, was different. To the surprise of all, the guest of honor was Kris Kringle himself. I thought to myself, "Now we're talkin'!"

As cubs, we formed a long blue line from the front of the hall to the rear. Much to my dismay, some anal scout leader desired organization and felt the need to say, "Line up by alphabetical order!" Back to the end of the line I went, and I was not too happy about it, for originally I had gained pole position.

It was a big moment for each of us. We had a direct pipe line to the Big Guy himself. I want to re-emphasize that as a group of young boys, we were stunned. And me? When I finally was permitted to hop up on Santa's lap, my emotions went through the roof, nearly knocking off the sled and each reindeer.

Why? Well it was at that very moment I had an epiphany. Having looked at Santa's left hand when he helped me climb to his lap, I noticed his wedding ring was identical to Pop's, a shiny gold band with a diamond upon it. I looked into Santa's eyes to compliment him on his choice of jewelry when …ZAP! I realized *Pop was Santa!*

It's important here that I'm clear. I did not for a second think, "Oh my…my father is pretending to be Santa Claus." I was thinking, "Holy smokes! *Pop is Santa…the real Santa!*"

I was on Cloud Nine. Nevertheless, I retired from scouting anyway five months later after a camping trip. The fact that the showers were cold put me over the edge. I am proud of one thing, however. That night back in December I never once blew his cover.

Oh! Then there's this: Remember in the beginning when I mentioned how some folks influence us? I am proud to report that I have assumed the role of our community's Santa Claus each year.

Pop died in February of 1984, but stories about him abound. This last one is my favorite. It was and still is a game changer. It might be the very reason I wanted to be a dad and a teacher.

Baseball was a common thread in our family and still is. Pop was the forerunner planting the seeds. My brothers were excellent players largely due to our father's coaching, while I enjoyed playing and coaching as well. Our daughter Ashton, named for our mom, was the only girl in our town's boys baseball league. Thanks to that experience and the coaching she received from Rupert, my Best Man, she later excelled in her teens as a softball player. Now we have a grandson who is following in his great grandfather's spikes. I am anxious to watch him play each season, for he seems to get better and better.

One family baseball story in particular not only teaches a lesson, but also sums up the wisdom of our father. I learned it the hard way.

I remind you that family legend has it that Pop was a baseball junky and a better-than-average player in his day. His were the days of Babe Ruth and Ty Cobb, and in his small town he was actually compared to them. In retrospect, that's probably not a big deal since I was named for Giants superstar Willie Mays, and nothing ever came of that. Both facts just add to the story.

Not long after Pop hung up his spikes, he realized he enjoyed passing along his love and respect for the game through coaching. However, to the surprise of no one in our family, "Coach" brought along with him a few of his own rules. Pop was old school before "old school" was identified.

One such rule was "No player swims on the day of a game." We all honored his request and obeyed...except once. When I was a left-handed sixth grade pitcher for the Warminster Little League Cardinals, I opted to go swimming one hot summer day in a local tributary that eventually led to the Delaware River. I was certain he would smell no chlorine upon me, so that made my infraction impossible to detect. After all, what else could give me away?

That evening I was scheduled to pitch against a weaker opponent. I knew that. Everyone on the team knew that. It was another reason I dared to break Pop's rule. The Dodgers couldn't hit a baseball if it was the size of a watermelon.

When the teams took the field, Cardinals versus Dodgers did not go well from the beginning. After one marathon inning, we were already losing by a several runs. Not pitching well, I was nearly out of gas. My tank was on "empty".

The second inning was more of the same, and it was then Pop calmly approached the umpire and spoke to him quietly. All of us knew he requested a time out. We didn't know the rest. A time out was granted, and he approached me on the mound.

When he arrived, he did two things I will never forget. Following baseball tradition, the infielders and my catcher circled the two of us on the mound to listen. To our surprise, Pop then indicated that he wanted all of the team in on this meeting. He not only called the outfielders to the mound, he signaled to our teammates on the bench that he wished them to be among us as well. This is what they heard as Pop spoke quietly:

"You went swimming today. Right?" It was one of those made-for-movie moments when the audience is permitted to hear crickets and a soft breeze passing by. Maybe a dog barked in the distance.

I looked down at my feet and spoke the only word I could say to my coach and my father, for both of them were in attendance.

"Yup."

Pop came back with the two words that not one of us ever expected. Nor will we ever forget them [evidently], for the moment's been recalled at my expense at many reunions since.

"Keep pitching." With that, he put his arms around the bench warmers and walked away.

I'd like to say our opponents smacked me around like a *birthday piñata* that game, and share how my teammates rallied to score enough runs to still win. Such an ending would have been nice, but it's not what happened. What *did take place* on that baseball field that evening was a handful of boys witnessing an important lesson being taught by a very insightful teacher.

Thanks, Pop, for everything.

TIME TRAVELERS

❧

"She knows my name," he thought.
"She actually knows my name!"

GARY ASHTON SUSPECTED THAT ATTENDING his high school reunion for the first time in forty years would be a social challenge. Despite fond memories of several former classmates, throughout all those years he had been in contact with only Glenn, and he wasn't attending the reunion!

When October 18th rolled around, Gary felt a little awkward as the evening unfolded. He and a one-time girlfriend spent much of the evening together. It seemed Adonika had been looking for him; waiting for him. He didn't think it was just his imagination.

During various stages of the reunion, the two were often side-by-side among old friends with whom they shared many secrets back in the day. As he moved about the large, ostentatiously-decorated banquet room, she followed, politely mingling with some other fellow graduates who at one time were simply pleasant acquaintances. In each category were teammates as well as students they befriended in band, chorus, theater, and clubs. A few had been pranksters while others had been saints.

Tom was one of the captains on the football team our senior year, and he enjoyed regaling how he and some buddies wrapped the Homecoming Queen's car in toilet paper until it looked like a mummy. "It was all good, clean fun. No one was hurt, and no property was damaged, but Sue was not too happy." The car prank in question was even memorialized in their high school yearbook.

On one side of the hall, hundreds of photos were shared bulletin-board style for all to see. Among the pictures, too, were decades-old news articles, sports reportage, and a smattering of obituaries.

As Gary passed them by, Kirk and Will teased each other about high school baseball days. "If you could hit, Kirk, we might have been a powerhouse!"

"Sure. And if you didn't walk so many batters, we might have won more than five games!" Jocks were the same everywhere.

All in all, it was a pleasant autumn evening; perhaps the last of Indian Summer. Driving into town earlier, Gary noticed the bulk of the colorful leaves that once painted the local landscape had fallen to the ground. Breezes had scattered most of the area's crimson and yellow maple leaves, and the rain that was forecasted would finish the job.

Before their four-course meal, there was a benediction and a moment of silence was respectfully requested for all of their deceased classmates. "I'm glad I wasn't responsible for any of that," Gary added to the table's conversation. "That would be awkward for me to do."

The vast banquet hall provided a wonderful space for the 500 classmates who attended Bogart High in 1965. The first hour was dedicated to arrival and registration where "Wildcats" were presented their nametags affixed to their senior yearbook photos. Dinner was served to groups of eight upon white linen tablecloths accented by burgundy napkins, all of it corresponding perfectly with their high school colors.

"Someone paid attention to details," people acknowledged to one another. "Such a wonderful presentation!"

Not only were the meals and desserts served in a timely fashion, to the approval of many they were quite delicious. Music played as everyone dined, and all of it was followed by dancing.

To Adonika, all of the evening was passing much too quickly. Leaning toward her boyfriend of years ago, she commented, "I know time flies when we have some fun, but I wish the night would last longer."

Chatting, mingling, and dining was agreeable, but for Gary the thought of time presented a different concern. He wasn't the first to consider departure, for dozens of classmates had already said their goodbyes. A two-hour drive back home could not be ignored especially since the weather was inclement. Gary was quite content with the evening's events, but Adonika craved for more.

An innermost piece of him, however, mirrored his ex-girlfriend of years ago. He, too, was a closet romantic and actually had emotional feelings about their reunion. She was still a beautiful woman, as were many in attendance that night. "Adonika is proof positive," he let himself think, "that time is not always so kind to all of us."

For but a moment, it saddened him that some of his class-mates might not ever see each other again. When he con-sidered how much everyone seemed to enjoy the sharing of fine food, sincere and interesting conversations, and several good laughs laced with fond memories, he hoped it would happen again. But as he stood canvassing that huge room full of people, suspecting some members of his high school class might never again experience the pleasantries they all were sharing, he suffered a pang in his heart.

After all, everyone had been entertained by good music and, despite their age, a few even dared to dance a time or too. Seeing their smiles helped balance Gary's emotional scale. He simply shrugged his shoulders and attributed his momentary somber thoughts to his career experiences that anchored him with realism.

Adonika's favorite part of their storybook night was dancing in the arms of her old flame. Until she learned he was attending their 40th high school reunion, she had not realized Gary was the sole candle she had never cared to extinguish. It shouldn't have mattered, but in her eyes that

October night he managed to impart a presence she couldn't ignore. The sound of his voice, like his scent, was subtle and to die for.

A taller blonde, she enjoyed it when they looked into each other's eyes. Albeit brief glances, perhaps a subconscious effort so gossips would begin no new stories, she wondered if Gary might still possess a candle all his own. Such a thought stirred inside of Adonika a pleasant emotion. There were nosey classmates in attendance that night who knew of her marital status, and she wanted to keep their tongues from wagging.

"Some things just never change," she whispered to herself as one class gossip walked away after she finished her social interrogation. Their entire conversation had been exchanged under the disguise of a friendly, caring chat, an art form that polishes with age.

Again they danced. "Don't you think this has been a wonderful night?" she inquired as they slowly moved about the floor.

"It's been great," he replied as he nodded a hello toward one of the men who grew up in his neighborhood. "There's Dave," he whispered softly. "I didn't know he was here. There are so many folks to see." His mind drifted as he recalled the two-story tree house they once constructed together from scraps of wood discovered at various job sites. "We used to do everything together."

"Make sure you go speak to him," she insisted in a supportive tone. At least she sounded encouraging. What she really wanted was more of her dance partner's attention. As they danced a second time, she purposely attempted to hold him closer. Gary appeared a bit uncomfortable, but she wrote it off as her imagination.

Such pleasure and excitement over the course of the night made saying goodbye to everyone a plaintive sensation. The emotion was similar to what she felt whenever she heard the call of a loon upon the lake near her childhood home in Maine. However, unlike that loon which shared its song with everyone near the lake on those misty evenings, Adonika kept her feelings within.

After an abundance of handshakes and hugs at night's end, Gary Ashton began to step outside through the club-house's magnificent French doorway. Adonika suggested that he should stay until morning. "Surely you're a bit tired," she imparted while brushing an invisible hair from his shoulder. Gary assured her he was fine, adding he needed to be back home in the morning, for he had some pending commitments.

"It was wonderful seeing you again after all these years," Adonika told him softly and leaned in to kiss his cheek. At that he blushed and assured her that he had enjoyed seeing her again as well.

"You have my email address, so I hope you'll stay in touch."

He promised that she'd hear from him soon and hugged her one final time. She watched him walk into the night and disappear around a corner of the brick, two-story clubhouse.

He wasn't alone as he drove north up the darkened highway. His private thoughts provided plenty of company. After leaving The Club at Carversville, the road had quickly become rural. Miles of yellow line stretched out ahead of him, and for part of the drive he kept his window partially down in an attempt to revive himself with fresh air. At a stop sign in Rivers Edge, he thought he heard a solitary loon.

Never one to drive too fast, it was natural for him to settle in and recall in detail all that the class had shared. He smiled as he recalled the Gag Awards distributed for such things as wildest story, sauciest wardrobe, and most humorous necktie or socks.

Suppressing it for miles, the one memory which eventually surfaced was the feel of her body close to his. All these years later, they still seemed to be a perfect fit. Adonika had easily out done him and most other folks in terms of remaining in good physical condition, and he admired her for that. He thought about how, as they danced together, he considered her dress to be provocative and how the material of her navy blue dress was so smooth to his touch.

For reasons only he understood, he was bothered by recalling such details. Something about it was not right. As he said earlier, he did have commitments although he chose not to elaborate. He didn't want to deal with the reactions of others. As the miles passed, Gary wondered just why that mattered so much. Then to himself he admitted the obvious. "Among other reasons, she married. That's why."

When he agreed to attend their reunion, he had not known she would be there as well. Had he considered the possibility? Yes. Was he hoping she'd attend? Yes, but because he had a commitment to honor, he should not have been thinking about the possibility of seeing her at all. As ten miles became twenty, he was unable to stop replaying their reunion in his mind.

Over and over the evening was revisited as he slowly drove up a stretch of northern highway, passing trees that had lost more leaves than those he left behind. In his headlights, the few remaining leaves he could see upon the branches were slipping away like the minutes had done throughout the evening. Rain began to fall harder, and *more* leaves flew across his path. They distracted him and made concentration more difficult.

Forty-five minutes passed when his reveries were abashed. Flashing headlights were spotted in his rearview mirror from quite a distance. Curiosity took a hold, and he deliberately slowed his driving even more. Eventually the vehicle behind him trailed by only a few car lengths.

With some trepidation, he drove to the side of the road. With the exception of a small diner, he could not recall having recently passed any houses, stores, or restaurants, and it made him feel a bit vulnerable. Scenes from the big screen raced through his mind, scenes where a victim's head was split by a hatchet-wielding wild man. Perhaps the figure partially silhouetted by its headlights would be a Good Samaritan. Perhaps he was an officer carrying a message meant solely for him. What might this person want? He also briefly questioned his decision to pull off on the shoulder at the side of the road.

With the rain letting up he was able to see, and was semi-relieved to note that the driver in the headlights behind him was certainly not a man. A taller woman had extricated herself from the quietly-idling car behind him, and she was wearing a blue dress.

As she approached, Adonika popped open an umbrella. It was then that Gary recognized her provocative, runway-model walk. To him, she had grown to be even more attractive than when last they met decades ago, and having such a thought made Gary a trifle uncomfortable. Was there a second candle flickering as well?

Once within earshot, in a voice consisting of much surprise he asked, "What in the world are you doing out here on such a night? Why did you follow me?"

As if to avoid his inquiries, she adamantly replied, "Gary, it's beginning to rain even harder." Adonika looked over his shoulder at his car. "Let's pick a car, get out of the rain, and talk."

Both vehicles were well off the highway and would not have obstructed any traffic that might have come along. The pair opted to sit in her newer, roomier rental, a Chrysler product which oozed class and style. She had been correct about the downpour. So intense was the rain that it nearly drowned out their attempts at conversation.

"I'm certainly glad we got in the car when we did!" she loudly announced in hopes of initiating some dialogue. She sensed a hesitancy on his part and wondered if Gary was holding back for a reason.

After a moment, he turned in her direction and repeated his question. "Adonika, why exactly did you follow me out here?"

She shrugged her shoulders at first, but then got to the heart of the matter. "I was so happy to see you, and I wasn't ready for our night to end." She hesitated and postured her index finger to indicate she had more she wanted to say. "As I tried to catch up to you, I anticipated your questions and rehearsed what I wanted to tell you." She paused again, but this time he didn't wait for her to continue.

Curious to know, he replied in a tone which hinted he had found humor in what she had just told him. "Well what did you come up with? I would really like to know."

"My thoughts were almost like those of the Adonika you knew back during our school days together when we were a couple." She shifted upon her plush, gray seat. The steering wheel pressed against her left leg and made her uncomfortable. She ignored it at first but then slid toward him. "I have to be honest. When I learned from Debby you were in attendance tonight I became excited." Immediately she could tell by his expression that he was flattered, but at the same time there was just something in his countenance barely discernable that hinted he was a tad uncomfortable, too.

"So you hopped into this car of yours…"

"It's not mine," she interrupted. "It's a rental."

He continued. "So you hopped into this rental after I left because…"

Again she interrupted. "I hopped into this car simply because I wanted to spend more time catching up with you, no pun intended." Gary noted she sounded flustered, even a little exasperated. "I'm interested to learn more about what has become of you after all these years." Another brief pause and then, "Throughout the night you really haven't told me much."

"Adonika, we chatted throughout the evening..."

"...but all of that information was so superficial. There were so many interruptions."

He nodded in agreement. "There were a lot of people to visit." Now it was his turn to pause, not for effect but to truly collect his thoughts. He stared out into the dark, rainy night through the windshield. "We are part of a huge graduating class. What was the number? 512? And we had only three or four hours to visit before, during, and after dinner." He looked back at her in hopes that he was making sense. "In my opinion, we did very well in the reuniting department." Then he smiled. "We even squeezed in a few dances."

"*Two...two dances*," she thought to herself. Adonika didn't quite know what to say. Since they had not been with each other nor spoken with each other since high school, she was eager to learn more about his past. What frustrated her was that he appeared to be perfectly satisfied with the little she had shared with him.

Then she realized, "*I don't even know if he's married!*" There was so much more she wanted to know. For her own part, she did choose to not play all of her cards during the reunion.

She had not shared any information that indicated she was nearing the end of her marriage to a man in Philadelphia. Nevertheless, she had made up her mind that she was not to be denied the chance to exchange more of their respective stories. She chose another approach.

"I would really enjoy a coffee right now," she announced. She saw him lean back as if startled. "While driving out here after you, I noticed an old-fashioned diner a few miles back…"

"…complete with neon lights, white panels, and chrome. I saw it, too," he replied. "Open twenty-four hours." Much to her surprise he asked, "May I buy you some breakfast?"

His willingness to reverse directions gave Adonika hope. "*Now we're getting somewhere,*" she thought, but aloud she countered with, "Yes! That would be wonderful." Then she added a lie. "I spoke with so many folks this evening that I took very little time to eat."

"Okay then," he consented. "To the diner we go!" He knew she lied, but he didn't have the heart to tell her. She had spoken to everyone throughout the course of their meal. Nevertheless, Gary jogged back to his Buick and began following her back toward Carversville.

As he followed her, the night's rainfall once again intensified. Hating the storm and not sure he was doing the right thing by appeasing Adonika, he began experiencing some anxiety. A beautiful evening and reunion were taking on another dynamic. "I probably should not have agreed to this," he said aloud to no one. He scolded himself for his decision.

Miles passed, and the rain fell harder, pelting his wind-shield with larger drops that splattered as if he had been purposely targeted. He groaned audibly, and his grip upon the wheel could get no tighter. Despite it all, his mind drifted again to their distant past.

Gary and Adonika met as younger teens when seventh and eighth graders were labeled *junior high school students.* In those years, he believed very few students knew his name, and but it seemed everyone knew Adonika. Taller than some boys and possessing both a beautiful smile framed by long, blonde hair, Adonika turned a lot boys' heads. There's no denying that her beauty put her on nearly everyone's social radar; however, it was her friendly demeanor that gained her notoriety. She was friendly to girls and boys alike. Few were the lunch tables that did not enjoy her company.

As he fought with his defroster, Gary recalled the first time she spoke to him during Mrs. Bloss's math class. Or was it her science class? Always great with numbers, Adonika was often permitted to tutor the mathematically challenged. Gary was one of those. Unbeknownst to him, he had been assigned by his teacher, and Adonika approached him gently and with respect.

In a voice almost angelic, Adonika whispered, "Hi, Gary. That stuff is awfully hard sometimes. Can we work on it together?" Momentarily he stopped breathing while fumbling with some variant of "Are you kidding?"

"She knows my name," he thought. "She actually knows my name!" Then she smiled. He was smitten. Gary never forgot that day, right down to the smallest detail. She was wearing a herring bone jumper over a light blue, short-sleeve blouse. These were memories that seemed to help loosen his grip on the steering wheel, and apparently the downpour had relented as well.

As romances and courtships go, theirs was fleeting. Not quite a meteor across the night sky, perhaps it was more of a long-lasting comet. It was there for a brief time for all to see, and then it disappeared. As he once admitted to a friend, "If gossip was a pond, our breakup didn't cause a ripple."

Continuing through the wet, dark night toward the diner, he recalled how throughout high school they rarely saw each other. The school was a cavernous facility by design. It was a flat, brick-and-cement, one-story product of the Sixties. To many students, it resembled a spider web in which under classmen were destined to suffer at the hands of juniors and seniors. As it turned out, Gary and Adonika shared not one common class the entire four years at Bogart.

Yet the one place he did see her with some regularity was in the bleachers at varsity baseball games. As a sophomore, he was talented enough to earn the varsity coach's nod as the team's starting first basemen. He was certain she noticed him, but he never figured out who it was that she was there to see. As they ate dinner during the reunion he finally asked her.

"I was watching you," she replied matter-of-factly. "*It was always you,*" she added silently in her head.

Throughout their high school years, aided by her good looks and dynamic personality, Adonika blossomed even more. She met new people and formed new friendships. Unbeknownst to most of the student body and faculty, she even managed to excel at modeling on weekends. Only her best friend Debby was aware of her modeling and only because Debby's older sister was employed by Adonika's agency. Over the years, Debby proved to be a wonderful confidante and keeper of secrets both large and small.

It spoke volumes of Adonika that the money she earned as a teen was voluntarily presented to her parents to supplement their income. At least that was her intention. Years later she learned her dad was a well-respected, highly-decorated officer in the Merchant Marine, commanding a decent enough salary to support his wife and children. His earnings helped make lengthy absences at sea more tolerable.

Adonika's mother kept a steady job, too. She was a juvenile officer for the local schools. At the end of her senior year in high school, Adonika discovered just how thrifty Mom was with a penny. Upon her high school graduation, her proud mother presented Adonika with a savings account all her own. In it was every penny she had earned while modeling.

At nineteen, while a hostess at an upscale restaurant Adonika caught the eyes of many a male customer. One in particular, a bit older than she, began dining in her restaurant regularly. In the brief moments a hostess takes to seat her guests, a lot can be learned. She learned he was single and noted that often he was eating alone. Too, she liked that he was a construction worker, self-employed, and relatively successful as evidenced by his multiple vehicles. Finally he asked her for a date. Adonika consented despite her mom's mild concern regarding the modest difference in their ages.

Dating eventually led to marriage. It was a pleasant and modest occasion attended by both families and a smattering of friends. Dad walked his beautiful daughter down the aisle, she in her gown of white satin and lace, and he in his uniform looking proud and handsome.

Gary heard all of this during the reunion dinner and a couple of drinks. It struck him that his former sweetheart had much to share. Earlier that evening as she talked over dinner, at some point he wondered, "Where's her husband?" He chose not to ask her thinking it might have been awkward.

The neon lights were aglow! Upon seeing her sitting in the diner's parking lot, he forgot about the reunion. The place seemed to glow bright red and orange against the dark of night. Carefully he pulled in next to her car. Opening her door she teased, "Man, you are a slow driver!"

"If I drove any faster, you might never have caught up with me an hour ago!" He took her arm and led her inside.

They chose a booth in a corner. Easily they were the best-dressed customers in the diner at that moment. For a while, they chatted about inconsequential topics.

"Is this rain ever going to let up?"

"I hope so for your sake," she replied. "Driving in the rain can be exhausting."

By the time their pancakes arrived, it was shortly after midnight. As a courtesy the waitress asked, "Would either of you like a refill on your coffee?" They both accepted her offer.

Once they were alone and they began to enjoy their breakfast, Adonika asked Gary to tell him about his home. She wanted to know about Butler and wanted him to describe it. He did the best he could considering it was a small town in a rural area.

"We depend a lot on tourism, I guess." He proceeded to tell the history of the lake region up north and how things were pretty quiet during winter months. "Weekends stay busy thanks to snowmobiles, ski runs, and hunting, but all in all things quiet down after December First."

As he was finally providing some of the information she desired, Gary thought he heard a siren off in the distance. She noticed how quickly he turned to pay attention and how his interest in her seemed to abate.

She tried to sound concerned as she wiped her mouth with a paper napkin and said, "In this bad weather, I wonder if there was an accident nearby."

No sooner were the words out of her mouth, and the first siren was echoed in the night by a second. There was no doubt that both emergency vehicles were headed in the direction of the diner. As they ate, eventually a moment arrived when Gary clearly began paying more attention to the events outside than he was paying to Adonika, and it bothered her.

In her mind, Adonika began hearing an alarm of her own, a warning of sorts. Casting caution to the wind she grew bold. As he stared out the plate glass window she asked, "Gary, why don't you wear a wedding ring?"

Simultaneously there was a sense of urgency inside the diner, and all of it was not Adonika's. At the exact moment she blurted the one question she needed to ask, the diner's short order cook and its dishwasher raced outside through the metal-framed, glass front door! Together they hopped into a green pick up truck, and a round, blue light atop its cab temporarily painted the diner inside and out. They sped off to the south. Her question seemed to hang in the air.

"Horrible accident up the road toward Carversville," the waitress informed them. Gary was looking out the plate glass window as the young woman explained to them what had transpired. "Gene Krause and Scott Mead are firemen, so you are lucky you have your pancakes."

Gary overlooked the young lady's attempt at humor. He knew she meant nothing by it. As if ignoring Adonika, he suddenly stood and clumsily bumped the edge of their table while reaching into his pocket for cash. As quickly as he could, he handed the waitress a twenty-dollar bill along with a ten.

In the most sincere voice that he could summon he announced, "I'm sorry, Miss, but I have to go. I hope there's enough here for our breakfast and your tip." That being said, he walked quickly toward the very same exit.

About to leave, he heard Adonika's voice for the very last time. She was yelling.

"Gary, where are you going? What are you doing?" Sounding greatly agitated she boomed, "Are you going to just leave me here alone?"

He stopped momentarily, turned 180 degrees, and saw her alone in the booth. He understood the look of astonishment upon her beautiful face, and it made him feel terrible he was leaving her there.

"I *have* to go, Adonika. I simply must go. It's my job to help them if I can." He knew that she still didn't understand. How could she? She was clueless about this part of his life. Gary Ashton, the man she loved since high school, now had to tell her all she wanted to know...and *didn't* want to know... in that instant.

Two ambulances screamed by as if in a race. Their presence added to the tension and excitement of the moment. Customers' noses were temporarily glued to the diner windows as they witnessed each emergency vehicle passing them by. As the noise crescendoed, the large, yellow ambulances nearly drowned out the last words he ever spoke to his high school flame.

"I'm a priest, Adonika, and I really must go." Called by commitment, he trotted into the rain-soaked darkness. For the second and final time he was gone.

Will Wyckoff's first novel ***Birds on a Wire*** was published in 2012. Tis a *non-political* story about the power of family, friendship, and possible redemption. The tale recounts the efforts of fictional U.S. President Elijah Rittenhouse as he attempts to prevent the murder of his friend Eli Parks at the hands of a beautiful North Korean Assassin.

His second novel ***Rabbit Trails*** was published in 2015. Like his favorite book ***To Kill a Mockingbird,*** it is a young adult or "YA" novel. ***Rabbit Trails*** takes readers down Memory Lane as it recalls adolescent subjects such as constant bullying and unwavering friendship. This is a tale of a young man's quest for answers regarding his grandfather's mysterious disappearance and what he was able to discover .

Both books are available in the following manner:

1) WillWyckoff.com
2) Via Createspace e-store:
   www.createspace.com/3727575 & www.createspace.com/5446325
3) Kindle
4) Amazon Books
5) Barnes & Noble or...
6) Contact Will Wyckoff to order a personalized, autographed copy via Facebook or his email address: upstairs@ptd.net

Manufactured by Amazon.ca
Bolton, ON